DARING QUEST

"Why have you come here, Crutcher?" Po-ah-Key asked. "What is it you want from us now—after all this time?"

"I want to talk to Thumb—under a flag of truce," he said.

"He will not hear of it," Po-ah-Key objected.

"Make him!" Crutcher shouted.

"I make Thumb do nothing. He is a wild thing. He will kill you, no matter what," Po-ah-Key said.

"You tell Thumb that I want the boy. He has a mother. A mother who lost her husband and wants her only son back." Crutcher continued, "Tell him I will come down tonight—unarmed."

"But he is Thumb's son!" Po-ah-Key pointed out.

"No. Thumb may say it, but it is not true."

"You are a brave man, Crutcher. Reckless. But what if *I* had chosen to kill you?"

When there was no answer from Crutcher the Indian realized that he had slipped away, probably preparing himself for the night's meeting.

In the distance Crutcher stood alone, his heart heavy. A time for dying had come upon them once more. And this time, one he loved would die.

FIVE FAST-ACTION NOVELS OF THE FRONTIER WEST

GHOST OF A GUNFIGHTER (559, $1.95)
by Wayne C. Lee
Dave Paxton finds himself in double trouble when he returns to Monotony to avenge his uncle's death and discovers the murderer is his look-alike.

MASSACRE AT WOUNDED KNEE (542, $2.50)
by Abby Mann
Spurred by the brutal killing of an old Indian, young radical leaders convince their fellow Indians to make a stand for their rights. They begin a peaceful hunger strike which ends in a violent, useless battle reminiscent of the age-old MASSACRE AT WOUNDED KNEE.

RIDE TO REVENGE (551, $1.95)
by Eric Allen
Jake Spaniard, a high-tempered young gunfighter from Whiskey Smith, killed his pa's murderer and is out to shoot the man who's tampering with his family's land.

RIFLES OF REVENGE (568, $1.95)
by Lewis B. Patten
Lucille Robineau seeks revenge against the "Cattle King" who caused her father to take his own life. She hires the meanest, deadliest man in town to shoot him dead with his quick-fire RIFLES OF REVENGE.

SHOWDOWN AT FIRE HILL (560, $1.95)
by Roe Richmond
After being forced to kill a bandit who'd once been his friend, Ranger Lashtrow wanted to lay down his guns. But deadly gunnies wouldn't let him run away, and he knew, sooner or later, he'd be back behind a gun barrel—even if it killed him.

Available wherever paperbacks are sold, or order direct from the Publisher. Send cover price plus 50¢ per copy for mailing and handling to Zebra Books, 21 East 40th Street, New York, N.Y. 10016. DO NOT SEND CASH!

WILDERNESS TRACK

BY OWEN G. IRONS

ZEBRA BOOKS

KENSINGTON PUBLISHING CORP.

ZEBRA BOOKS

are published by

KENSINGTON PUBLISHING CORP.
21 East 40th Street
New York, N.Y. 10016

Printed in the United States of America

One

The ragged line of horsemen wound across the empty desert flats. The sun was white overhead, brilliant in an utterly clear sky, and the men squinted against the day, searching the long empty land of amber-hued sands and rust-colored rock. In the far distance, through the shimmering heat waves, they could see the indistinct forms of the chocolate-colored mountains. There was nothing else to see; nothing else moved across the broad expanse of desert waste but the lone high vulture, black against the fire of the sky.

Sergeant Wren lifted a stubby finger toward the buzzard, but the lieutenant only nodded. He had seen it half an hour earlier.

Lieutenant Aston's broad, determined face was coated with yellow dust, streaked by lines of perspiration as Wren glanced at the officer.

None of them had spoken since Riodoso Wells, the last watering hole this side of Cheer.

They rode like phantoms—the only sounds the jingling of bridle chains, the creaking of leather, the blowing of the horses as they wove across the playa. Dust streamed out behind them, into the yellow sky. Wren cursed silently, profusely as he saw the second buzzard climb lazily into the southern sky.

They came on it shortly before dusk. The high, frail clouds which had gathered to the west were a deep purple. The sands reflected this purple coloration. Shadows gathered in the deep gorges and stretched out toward the flats as Lieutenant Aston raised his hand, halting his men.

"Damn," Sergeant Wren muttered, though he had expected it all along, hoped for nothing more.

Aston shook his head wearily, wiping his hat band with his scarf. He glanced at Wren and started his buckskin down the long slope.

The railroad train lay wrecked in the canyon below them like some gigantic dead insect. The locomotive had derailed and lay on its side in a deep gouge it had slashed in the earth.

The Pullman cars had been torched and gutted. The scent of dead smoke hung in the sunset air. Baggage was strewn across the rough landscape. A woman's blue dress hung on a clump of thorny mesquite. There was a set of broken dishware scattered everywhere. A stovepipe hat rested beside the body of a drummer.

From the look of determination on the little man's face, Wren figured he had died fighting.

Sculls was walking along the cars, peering inside now and then, but he shook his head as Lieutenant Aston glanced up at the trooper.

The engineer was beneath the locomotive's drive wheel, his arm torn off. Wren turned away and walked toward the back of the train where Aston stood, his head hung with concern.

"Anything?" he asked Wren.

"No, sir," the big-shouldered sergeant answered.

"Sculls?"

"Nothing, sir. They broke into the freight car. Both guards are dead. Both scalped." He spat. "Safe's empty."

Aston nodded slowly. The night was coming in rapidly, the air chilling against his sweat-dampened uniform shirt.

"But I found this," Sculls said.

He handed the article to Aston, who turned it over slowly. A child's hand puppet with goggle eyes and a petrified, toothy smile. Aston looked up again at Sculls, an unspoken question in his eyes.

"No, sir. I didn't find no kid inside."

"Wren!" Aston shouted louder than necessary. "Get up a burial party."

Wren nodded, perplexed. The lieutenant walked the length of the train once more as Wren and the troopers watched him.

"Think it was Thumb, Sarge?" Tyler Winston asked.

"It was," Wren replied shortly. Winston was young, very young and his pale face reflected the fear he felt in the pit of his stomach.

"He'll be riding high and handsome now," Sculls grunted. His dark eyes were thoughtful. Wren had never liked this long-faced, swarthy trooper, yet he could find no real reason for feeling that way.

"Let's dig us some graves, Sculls," Sergeant Wren said.

Sculls nodded slowly. There was something working behind those dark eyes, but he said nothing. He turned on his heel, walking with Tyler Winston to the low sandy knolls beyond the tracks.

Lieutenant Aston again examined the rails which had been pried loose, derailing the train. An iron bar still lay nearby.

So Thumb was back with his renegades. They had expected it, but not so soon. They had known that the Mexican army would mount a full-scale offensive designed to drive the Chiricahua warlord out of their country. And now he was back.

A flight of doves winged homeward across the purple skies. The red canyon walls cast deep shadows over the dead locomotive.

Aston, who had been crouched on his heels, rose, dusting off. He regretted what must be done now as much as he regretted anything his career had yet thrust upon him.

At Fort Bowie it would be his job to inform Colonel Blodgett that Thumb was back in the territory, and that the fifty thousand dollars in gold—army payroll money—had been taken from the freight car after the Apaches had massacred the train crew and passengers.

Aston tugged his hat down, looked once again at the child's puppet he still held in his hand, and strode back toward his men.

On the heels of that bleak information, Aston would have the unhappy duty of informing the colonel that Thumb had taken his grandson hostage.

Colonel Cleveland Hodgett was nearly fifty years old, with thirty years of army service behind him. His closely cropped silver hair was brushed stiffly back. A neatly trimmed silver mustache framed his narrow, purposeful mouth. His blue eyes were surprisingly mild, playing against the general toughness of his square face.

Hodgett had seen much in his fifteen years in the West, and some that touched his deep sense of humor which he rarely showed to his subordinates.

Now his eyes showed no softness, only a flint-hard resolve. Lieutenant Aston stood rigidly before his broad, uncluttered desk.

"You are sure it was Thumb, Lieutenant?" the colonel asked, drumming his fingers on the walnut desk.

"Yes, sir."

"Then he's well set up now, isn't he? With fifty thousand gold dollars—army dollars—to buy weapons and supplies."

The question demanded no answer. Aston only nodded absently. The colonel had turned to face the window. Across the parade ground "A" troop was standing morning inspection. Beyond the stockade walls, smoke rose lazily from the town of Cheer. Aston saw the colonel's jaw muscles tense and then relax and, as Hodgett turned to face the junior officer, a momentary weariness etched the colonel's face. He had pushed the thought aside, forced himself to do so, but now he asked with restrained forcefulness, "Aston, are you sure Richard was on that train?"

Frank Aston placed a hand inside his tunic and slowly removed the puppet, placing it on Colonel Hodgett's desk. The colonel stared at it as if it were Satan's own accusing finger, then his pale eyes lifted to Aston.

"Get Crutcher," he commanded.

"But, sir . . ." Aston balked. "Crutcher is . . ."

"Get Crutcher!" Colonel Hodgett repeated, and there was no questioning the order. Aston saluted, spun smartly on his heel and walked from the office. Wren was outside, waiting.

"Well?" the sergeant asked in that casual tone which sometimes irritated Aston, but which he now ignored.

"He wants Crutcher," Aston told him.

"Crutcher . . ." Sergeant Wren swallowed an oath, spat and shook his head. "I'll get half a dozen men," he said.

* * *

The soldiers, under Wren's directions, stormed through the Lucky Rover and the Showboat before finding Crutcher sagged over a round table at Arizona Sam's.

The bartender, a bald man named Peoples, glanced up at the blue-uniformed soldiers, his eyes wide with pained astonishment.

"You're going to wake him up?" Peoples asked.

"That's right."

Peoples turned, removed the mirror from behind the bar, took off his white apron and grabbed his hat, heading for the door. He was not alone.

Wren's men circled the small table which was damp with whisky-bottle rings. Crutcher was sprawled contentedly over the table, arms under his chin, eyes closed in deep sleep.

He was a tall, sandy-haired man with a slackness to his face from the drinking, but with purposeful lines under that slackness, hard cheek and jaw lines. The cheeks were hollow, cropping pale whiskers just now. His hair tumbled out from under his torn hat. He wore buckskins over a black shirt and a worn, blue Colt on his hip. As Sergeant Wren silently reached for the Colt, all hell broke loose.

Crutcher's hand shot out and locked on Wren's wrist with an iron grip. Crutcher mumbled without opening his eyes, "Get the hell away from me."

"Sure, Crutch." Wren withdrew his hand carefully.

"Hell—he's dead drunk, Sarge," a corporal named Benton muttered. "Why fool with him?"

Benton shoved a hand under Crutcher's arm and the tall man's eyes flashed open. A fist lashed out and took Benton flush on the jaw and the trooper thudded back against a table, scattering chips and glasses.

With a roar, Crutcher came to his feet, kicking his table aside. His blue eyes showed red fire; his hat spun off as he punched out at the soldier nearest him, knocking the soldier's head violently sideways.

The troopers ganged in on Crutcher now, leveling their best shots at him. Crutcher took a sharp left to the nose and blood began trickling from it, but he was in a fighting rage and he struck back left and right, sandy hair flying. A buckskin-fringed arm shot out and took a man on the point of the chin. Crutcher was knocked back against the wall by one of the troopers and, yelling savagely, came up with a chair, breaking it to kindling over a man's back.

"Crutch!" Wren called from behind him. "We only want . . ."

But at the sound of Wren's voice, Crutcher had spun and struck out with a left and a right. Wren was a big man and used to fighting and he managed to parry the first blow, but the second caught him on the jaw and Wren fought back angrily, a righteous indignation prodding him.

Wren waded in and took another shot, this one on the shoulder and he shot a right of his own into Crutcher's face. The lean man laughed, spat blood and backed off a few steps, throwing chairs at the pursuing soldiers.

"Crutch!"

"Get your dogs out of here, Wren! Disturbin' a man's beauty rest!"

A corporal lunged at Crutcher and was met by an outstretched boot which took him painfully on the kneecap. Crutcher shoved the trooper forward and down, the man's own momentum causing him to tumble to the sawdust-covered floor.

Wildly Crutcher fought his way across the room, blood running from mouth and nose, throwing chairs and tables in the path of the bloodied soldiers.

A cowboy peered in the door, shook his head and quickly backed out. A crowd had gathered at the window of Arizona's but now they scattered as Crutcher winged a chair at the window, splintering it in every direction.

"Damn . . ." a trooper with an already puffy, bloody face panted as he feinted left and then came in at Crutcher. Crutcher turned, ducked and came up with a right to the man's windpipe and he toppled forward, doubled up by the blow.

"Crutch!"

Crutcher again spun to the sound of Wren's voice, but this time he was met by the butt of Wren's pistol crashing down against his skull. The lights went on brilliantly for a spinning second, then went out, and Crutcher crumpled to the floor.

Wren, panting heavily, picked up Crutcher's hat and slapped it on the man's head as he hoisted him to a sitting position. He looked around at his troopers. Two of them were out cold, a third sagged against the wall, a silly smile on his unconscious features.

"Give me a hand," Wren puffed.

With Benton, Wren dragged Crutcher outside, through the crowd of onlookers, and together they tossed Crutcher into the horse trough.

Wren dunked him twice, put Crutcher's hat back on his head and stood him up.

"Can you walk?" he demanded.

"Hell, yes," Crutcher drawled.

"Colonel Hodgett requests your presence."

Crutcher's horse, a squat, scarred-up buckskin was standing at the rail, untied, and Crutcher was helped into the saddle. Then, with a guard of battered, bloody soldiers, he was escorted to the fort.

The guard at the gate saluted smartly and then gawked at the incoming bloody procession. He asked the last man through—the one with the torn shirt and bloody scalp, "Apaches?"

"Crutcher," the trooper mumbled around a swollen tongue.

Two

Crutcher's head was ringing and there was a dull stabbing pain low on his neck, but he felt well enough. He watched the commandant's office door for a long while, wiping the blood from his eyes, the corners of his mouth, feeling the dry wind off the Abrajos dry his buckskins.

Wren stepped out after a time and he nodded. "Come on in, Crutch."

Crutcher stepped stiffly from the saddle, tugging his hat low against the piercing glare of the desert sun. He went onto the porch, stamped the mud from his boots, and followed Wren's bulky figure into the square, shadowed room.

Colonel Hodgett was behind his desk and he glanced up as Crutcher came in. There was a competent-looking, dark-haired lieutenant Crutcher did not know standing nearby and

Hodgett introduced him.

"Crutcher, this is Lieutenant Aston."

Crutcher nodded and sat without being asked. Neither of the army men, he noted wryly, had offered a hand.

Aston was looking at him with an appraising eye and Crutcher didn't care for the conclusions the young lieutenant seemed to be drawing. He rubbed his whiskered chin, crossed his long legs and hung his battered hat on his knee, waiting.

"What is it, Colonel?" Crutcher asked shortly. "What is it that calls for setting your men on me like a pack of dogs, disturbing my peace?"

"Disturbing your drinking you mean," Hodgett said roughly. He rose from his chair and waved an intolerant hand.

"Well?" Crutcher asked again.

"Thumb. It's Thumb, Crutcher. He's back and blood hungry."

"Thumb." Crutcher nodded slowly, got to his feet and put his hat on. "I wish you luck."

"Crutcher!" Hodgett boomed.

"That what you call the tone of command, Colonel? Sorry—you don't see no blue shirt on my back, do you?" He smiled bitterly and half turned toward the door when he noticed the woman standing there.

Beautiful she was, and young. She had her hair coiled on her head. Dark hair, it caught the sunlight shining through the window and gleamed auburn. She had a proud cast to her eyes, but seemed pale now, grieved maybe.

"Sit down, Crutcher," the colonel said in a

softer tone. "Hear me out at least."

"All right," Crutcher answered the colonel, but he was watching the woman still, a faint smile turning up the corner of his broad mouth.

"This is my daughter, Mrs. Brown," Hodgett said.

"Ma'am," Crutcher nodded. He turned back to the colonel who was grim, hovering over his desk, fists planted on it.

"Thumb derailed a train yesterday down near Nopal. Killed eight folks. He made off with fifty thousand gold dollars, Crutcher."

Crutcher's eyebrows lifted slightly, but he said nothing.

He found himself still looking at the girl, who had her small hands clasped before her, her brown eyes intent on him.

"If you find Thumb, get that gold back— there's a twenty percent reward in it for you, Crutcher. Ten thousand gold dollars."

"Nope. Not interested," Crutcher answered, wagging his head.

"Ten thousand dollars, Crutcher! Enough to last you a lifetime."

"I believe I said I wasn't interested, Colonel," Crutcher said, and there was steel in his voice when he said it.

"If we don't capture Thumb," Lieutenant Aston put in, stepping toward Crutcher, his eyes pleading, "those eight dead folks will only be a scratch on the surface. He'll kill and kill again, Crutcher. And you know it!"

"I reckon he will, Lieutenant," Crutcher said

slowly, thoughtfully. "But it's the army's job to find Thumb, not mine. I've got my own business to take care of . . ."

"Your own business!" Aston exploded. "Damn, Crutcher! Do you put the bottle ahead of your fellow men?"

"Lieutenant, you don't know me well enough to talk to me that way." Crutcher's voice was hard, threatening. "No man knows me well enough to talk like that to me."

He glanced again at the woman and saw that her eyes were flashing with anger, her cheeks hot. Crutcher shook his head and nodded, "Now, if you'll excuse me." And he strode past the woman, through the open door.

"Father!" Rebecca Hodgett Brown stretched out a hand to her father, but the old man could only shake his silver head.

"Sir!" Aston interrupted. "If your daughter would only speak to Crutcher."

"I'll not beg before any man, nor will Rebecca!" Hodgett exploded.

"Not for Richard?" Rebecca demanded. "I'll beg for my son." She wrapped her shawl tightly around her shoulders and turned for the door, saying over her shoulder, "I'll get down on hands and knees before Crutcher if I have to. I'll crawl back to Cheer, begging him."

"Rebecca . . ."

But she was gone, stepping into the brilliant white sunlight, her eyes searching the parade ground. Finally she saw him, washing his face in the cool water of the well. A tall, filthy man

18

with the signs of liquor on his face, the mark of sin in his eyes. Rebecca summoned her courage, drew a deep breath and walked toward Crutcher, her shoulders erect.

"Ma'am." Crutcher looked up and nodded, wiping back his hair. There was an irritating smile on his broad mouth and Rebecca had to steel her nerves to look him in the eye.

"Sir, I've come to beg you to accept my father's proposal."

"I don't need the money, ma'am," Crutcher said, plopping his hat on his still damp hair. "Nor the aggravation."

"You don't understand," Rebecca said. She took his arm without meaning too, then withdrew her hand immediately, surprised at the hard muscle beneath the buckskin jacket.

She turned down her eyes and went on.

"They've got my son. Thumb has my Richard. He's only six years old, Mr. Crutcher. Just a little boy. He'll be frightened out of his mind. Terrified."

Crutcher looked at the woman whose shoulders now trembled slightly. Then he let his gaze seek the far mountains across the long white desert. When he spoke it was softly so that Rebecca had to lean forward slightly to catch his words.

"I imagine he'll be frightened for a time. But Thumb won't hurt him. Most often young boys like that are adopted, raised as Apaches. He'll be fed, clothed . . . I reckon that's all a youngster needs."

19

"He needs his mother!" Rebecca shouted, losing her control. "He needs love. It was terrible for him when his father died . . . he's not a strong boy," she went on.

"I reckon he'll grow stronger now," Crutcher said. Then he stepped into the saddle, watching Rebecca's face fall to misery, her lip trembling.

"What kind of man are you?" she shouted as he turned the buckskin and slowly rode toward the gate. She ran a step or two after the buckskin pony then crumpled up, falling to the dusty earth, tears streaming across her flushed cheeks.

Crutcher never looked back.

"Ma'am?"

Rebecca looked up into the broad, affable face of Sergeant Wren. Colonel Hodgett and Aston were rushing toward them across the yard.

"Are you all right?" Wren helped her to her unsteady feet and together they watched Crutcher's horse disappear through the gate, only a puff of dust left to mark his passing. The brilliant day was dying to sundown, long pennants of fiery cloud streaking the sky.

Colonel Hodgett gathered Rebecca in his arms and she said, nearly to herself, "What kind of man is that?"

"Don't worry, darling," Hodgett told his daughter. "We'll find the boy. We'll still go hunting Thumb. The army has its duty yet, with or without Crutcher."

"Certainly," she sniffed, smiling at her

father. She fumbled for and found a tiny handkerchief, and she dabbed at her eyes. Then she let her father lead her away as Lieutenant Aston and Sergeant Wren stood, still watching the gate.

"She's a fine, delicate woman," Aston said. "For a man like Crutcher to hurt her . . ."

"He didn't mean it," Wren said, turning to face Aston in the failing light. "You got to understand Crutcher—he's got reasons for acting the way he does."

"There's no excuse for cruelty," Aston replied stiffly. "We're better off without him, anyway. A man like that as scout could spell defeat for our mission."

"Sir," Wren said, "beggin' pardon, but I got to disagree. Crutcher's the only man who could mean success."

"I know he's familiar with the area . . ." Aston began.

Wren interrupted him.

"He knows every gulley, canyon and tinaja between here and Sonora, sir. He's hunted the Abrajos and trapped in the Chocolate range. He's one of the few men alive who could cross that desert in summer. He knows every critter, four-legged or two-legged, that wanders them wastes. And he knows fighting."

"But surely there are other scouts equally efficient, Sergeant," Aston objected.

"If there is, I never heard of him," Wren said, spitting on the ground. "And there damn sure ain't another one who's kin to Thumb."

"Kin?" Aston repeated as if he had misunder-stood.

"Kin," Wren affirmed. "Crutcher was married to Thumb's only sister."

Three

It was only two hours until dawn. The streets of Cheer were dead silent. Nothing moved across the desert beyond, nor was there a sound to be heard except a distant coyote baying at the late rising orange moon. A single light burned on the main street of Cheer.

Hal Peoples leaned heavily across the bar of Arizona Sam's. The place had been empty for hours and the chairs were stacked, the floor swept, the glasses washed. He sighed and spoke to the lone man sitting in the far corner.

"Crutcher—I need to sleep too. Won't you please go on home?"

Crutcher glanced up, saying nothing. Those icy blue eyes only stared out of the shadow cast by his hat brim. He turned a whisky glass in his hand. At his elbow was a bottle, but Crutcher hadn't touched his drink.

"What time is it, Hal?"

"Why, it's nearly four, Crutcher."

"Four?" Crutcher glanced at Peoples, puzzled. Then he lifted his glass to his lips. Without drinking from it, he put it gently down.

It was the woman, damn her. He kept seeing those dark, liquid eyes, that pleading mouth. Rebecca Brown was a proud, fine woman, yet she had come to him, begging. For love of her son.

Yet Crutcher knew better than anyone else that if Thumb was running, he could not be caught. Not until the Chiricahua wished to be caught. Then the hunter would become the slaughtered. Perhaps they believed that Thumb would not kill Crutcher, would in fact grant him favors . . . if the fools only knew, Crutcher thought grimly. There was no one in the territory Thumb hated more than Crutcher.

No. He decided suddenly, forcefully. No! What did he owe Hodgett, the army? Nothing at all. Why get himself killed on a fool's errand?

Thumb could not be caught. The gold could not be recovered. As for the kid . . . Crutcher shook the thought aside and downed his drink; it was sour, foul tasting.

Angrily he slapped the glass down and stalked from Arizona's into the biting cold air outside. He heard Peoples latch the door behind him and after a minute the lantern went out.

Wren had his troops fall out half an hour

24

before sunrise. Sculls and his cronies, White and Sam Denver, had volunteered. Benton was chosen personally by Wren as was the Kentuckian, Po Ferguson.

The scout would be Ivory Hunter. The old man was good, but his territory was to the north, higher up. He was known among the Utes and Arapahoe—had in fact lived with the Arapahoe for three winters, hunting with them. But he was not in the high mountains now . . . not among the Arapahoe.

The old man sat his jenny mule, long white hair flowing over his beaded buckskin shirt, Sharps rifle in his hand, watching as Sergeant Wren double checked the men.

Aston had not come out yet, but his black gelding stood saddled and ready. The lieutenant was getting his final instructions from Colonel Hodgett.

The horses stamped impatiently and blew steam against the cold gray of morning. Within hours it would be a hundred degrees on the searing flats. There were two horses carrying nothing but waterbags and Wren knew full well that even that would not be enough. There were waterholes scattered across the desert, seeps along the foothills and stony tanks called tinajas. But the seeps ran dry, the tinajas were fouled or empty as often as not. And without water there was no life on the desert.

Po Ferguson grinned broadly as Wren reached him with the ammunition sack.

"Sarge," the Kentuckian drawled. "My horse is already draggin' tail with all the lead I'm carryin'."

"Take 'em," Wren smiled, fishing a double handful of brass cartridges from the canvas sack. "You never know which one will be that last one."

Ferguson nodded and stashed the ammunition.

Sculls was standing, arms crossed, cursing the early hour. "Damn cold," he snarled as Wren handed him the extra shells.

Wren said nothing, but he wondered idly what a man like Sculls was doing on a dangerous volunteer mission.

Lieutenant Aston emerged from the colonel's quarters, stuffing a rolled-up chart into his tunic. He stood a moment, studying the men, watching the eastern horizon where already a pale yellow line showed. Then Aston stepped down off the porch, taking the reins of his black.

"Ready, Sergeant Wren?"

"Ready, sir."

"All right. Let's . . ." Aston fell silent, his foot in the stirrup, his leg frozen in the motion of swinging up.

The tall man sat his stubby buckskin, a Winchester slung across his back. He did not move for a long moment, then swinging down, Crutcher came up to where Aston was waiting.

"Am I still invited?" he asked.

Aston glanced back at the porch where Colonel Hodgett stood, frowning beneath his

26

silver mustache.

"Talk to the colonel."

Crutcher nodded, exchanged a brief, faintly amused glance with Wren, and strode toward the porch, leading his buckskin. "Morning," he said.

"You've changed your mind?" Hodgett asked.

"I have."

"Mind telling me why?"

"Are the terms still the same?" Crutcher asked, brushing aside Hodgett's query. The colonel nodded slowly, his mouth working against itself. Crutcher looked different—purposeful, perhaps. He had shaven and his blue eyes were clear.

"The terms are the same," Hodgett said.

"Good. The kid's name—what is it?"

"It's Richard."

"Got anything that belonged to him, colonel? Something he'll recognize as his?"

"There's this." It was Rebecca who said it. She came forward in a wrapper, her dark hair loose around her shoulders. She stretched out the toy in her hand and Crutcher took it, turning the goggle-eyed puppet over.

"He may need his memory jogged," Crutcher said. "Fear sometimes does funny things. I've seen it before."

Rebecca's eyes clouded with concern. She started to ask a question, but kept quiet. Crutcher tucked the puppet into his saddlebags and started to turn away. Then he paused.

"Ma'am—it may not be as fast as you'd hope.

27

It may be a time. A long time before we know."

Then he led his pony to where Aston waited before his men and swung up beside the lieutenant.

"You're going?" Aston asked in a brittle voice, his eyes straight ahead.

"I am."

Aston nodded and turned his horse toward the gate, calling back to Wren. "Let's move them out, Sergeant."

Crutcher sat his horse, hands resting on the pommel, watching the men ride past single file, trying to take stock of them with a single glance. There were only two of them he felt sure of—Wren and Ivory Hunter, whom he knew slightly.

Again Crutcher cursed himself for a fool, but he looked back toward the colonel's quarters and saw that fine, proud woman standing there, hope in her eyes, and he snapped the buckskin's head around, trailing the group out of Fort Bowie.

Dawn came in a blaze of color. Red arrows streaked out across the sky, painting the white sands below with reddish tints. The sun lay a line of beaten gold along the skyline of the Chocolate Mountains to the east and spattered the deep canyons with rich purple where the shadows still held.

Ivory Hunter moved up beside Crutcher as they rode southward. The old scout hooked his leg around his saddle horn as he rode and stoked up a stubby pipe, his long rifle crooked in his arm.

"This Thumb," Ivory asked, puffing gingerly, "will he run or fight, Crutcher."

"He'll run while he wants. Then he'll fight."

Hunter nodded, letting his clear gray eyes sweep the desert and the men who rode silently in front of them.

"Well," the old man said, "I've done me some chasin' and I've done me some fightin' as well."

"Apaches?" Crutcher asked.

"What's that? No," Ivory admitted, "I ain't fought the Apaches."

"It's different," Crutcher assured him. "Thumb won't come riding at us directly. He won't stand and fight. He'll peck away, his men rising up out of the sands and disappearing back into them. We'll spend our time chasin' ghosts. Then the ghosts will fight back."

Ivory nodded, pondering the guerrilla tactics he had heard described before. He had another thought and he asked Crutcher, "Think he'd trade the boy and the gold off? Say if we promised him freedom, or swapped horses and guns?"

"He won't trade," Crutcher said with a slight shake of his head. "Except to trade his bullets for our blood. He hates the whites with a blood lust, Ivory. And Thumb's no fool—he knows full well what that gold can buy."

"Don't sound like you figger we've much of a chance of accomplishing a thing—outside of

29

getting our own selves killed," Ivory said, his gray eyes twinkling with ironic amusement.

Crutcher locked eyes with the old man for a moment, saying nothing. Ivory Hunter nodded and let his jenny mule fall a few strides back. Then for a time he sat his saddle, studying the far distances and the tall sandy-haired man who rode in front of him.

Aston took off his hat and wiped the band once more. They rode through veils of heat waves like ghosts through an endless mirage of a sea. The black horse beneath him was coated with white alkali dust, and the grit clung to Aston's neck and face, whitening his eyebrows and dark mustache. He glanced back to see Crutcher coming up beside him.

"There's water for a night camp up along that wash, Lieutenant. No sense killing the horses or the men first day out."

"It's still early, Crutcher. We've plenty of ground to make up on the Chiricahuas."

"Sir—we could start these ponies runnin' if you like, but we wouldn't gain a mile on Thumb. He already knows we're after him, like as not, and he knows just where we are—even if we don't know where he is."

"You sound as if you don't expect to catch him at all, Crutcher," Aston snapped.

"Sir, I expect to meet up with Thumb. But I'd bet it'll be the Apaches who catch up with *us*."

Aston was silent. The heat was wringing his composure from him. As long as Crutcher was here, it was only common sense to utilize his skills.

"How far to that water?"

"Two miles or so." Crutcher lifted a finger toward the sandy hills beyond the dry arroyo. Aston nodded and swatted viciously at the gnats which were swarming over his face.

"What's his game?" Aston asked Wren after Crutcher had gone.

"Game?" the big sergeant asked. Wren shrugged.

"Why did he change his mind—he's related to Thumb, you say?"

"That's what they say," Wren answered. "I don't know much about it myself, except that Crutcher was married to an Indian woman."

Aston shifted in his saddle, turning back to watch Crutcher momentarily across his shoulder. There was something about the man that didn't set right. Besides the way he had treated Rebecca . . . something else.

They found the water hole two hours before sundown. Crutcher and Ferguson cleaned the shallow, stony basin of brush and sand while the others unsaddled.

"Bring the ponies down, will you, son?" Crutcher asked the Kentuckian.

"I'll do 'er," Ferguson nodded. The lanky trooper wore a constant grin and, Crutcher had noticed, he was seldom far from his rifle which was kept meticulously.

"How about we drink first, Crutcher?" a rasping voice interrupted.

It was the long-jawed man named Sculls.

31

Standing beside him were a red-headed soldier and a scar-faced man, Luke White and Sam Denver.

"Best let the horses have it," Crutcher said, standing, wiping the mud from his knees. "We won't get far without them."

Ferguson hadn't moved. His open eyes switched between Sculls and Crutcher who was pulling his hat on and stood holding his rifle by the barrel, butt on the ground.

"Get along now," Crutcher told Ferguson.

"I said we'd drink first, *squaw man*," Sculls said mockingly.

Crutcher froze, every muscle set. He stared at Sculls, measuring the man and the two beside him who held guns. Then Crutcher smiled, but it was not a pleasant smile.

"Get along Ferguson," Crutcher repeated.

"Maybe you didn't hear me," Sculls began, swaggering forward, but he had taken only two steps when Crutcher flipped up the butt of his Winchester and brought it down on the soldier's skull, dropping Sculls like a pole-axed steer.

"Maybe you didn't hear *me*," Crutcher said to the crumpled Sculls.

Luke White, smothering a curse, lifted his rifle toward his shoulder, but Crutcher had not forgotten the other two and White found himself looking at the muzzle of Crutcher's Winchester. He didn't like the looks of it or of the cool blue eye behind the sights. White put his rifle down gently and went to Sculls' side.

"What in the hell is going on here!"

Aston scurried up the slope, his shirt sleeves rolled up, fire in his dark eyes. He took the scene in at a glance. Sculls, clutching his bloody scalp, sat on the ground, Crutcher over him, rifle still on the other troopers.

"Crutcher—what in the hell is this?" Aston bellowed.

"Guess these three soldiers were kind of overcome by thirst," Crutcher said, smiling wryly. Aston was furious and he stepped to Crutcher, pushing away the muzzle of his Winchester.

"I can't have this. I won't have it, Crutcher!" He leveled his eyes on Crutcher and stepped closer to the scout. "Do you understand that? If you don't, it's only a day's ride back to Cheer, and you're welcome to leave."

"I'll stick," Crutcher said without further explanation.

Wren and Benton had come up to the water hole now, and the soldiers stood silently, watching. This was it, and sooner than they had expected. Who was to be in charge of this mission—Lieutenant Aston or Crutcher? Aston knew what their thoughts were and he thought he had made his point.

Yet Crutcher had not backed up a step, nor did Aston expect the tall man to.

Ferguson interrupted the long silence. He had the ponies with him and he asked, "Water the horses first, Lieutenant Aston?"

"Yes," Aston replied without turning from Crutcher. "Water the horses first."

Sculls had staggered to his feet and he glared at Crutcher with a ferocity that was animal. Crutcher glanced at the man, but only briefly.

"I'll take first watch," Crutcher said flatly, "up on the ridge there."

Aston said nothing, and Crutcher, snatching up a canteen, turned to climb the rocky, sand-colored ridge beyond the water hole.

It was rough going. But he had the canteen slung over his shoulder, his rifle dangling on a sling down his back, and after half an hour's clawing through mesquite and sage, up over rough, weather-bitten outcroppings, Crutcher found himself on a small ledge from which he could look for miles out over the desert.

Day was nearly done. A cookfire glowed dully in the army camp. Long shadows stretched out onto the flats. A quail sung from up along the sandy, dry wash. Crutcher removed his hat, raked back his sandy hair and took a deep cooling swallow of water.

The skies were fading to violet and, far off to the south, he could see the gleam of the railroad tracks where they hoped to pick up Thumb's trail.

Crutcher put down the canteen and sighed deeply. He hadn't wanted to start trouble with any of the soldiers—to fight effectively, any unit must be that: a unit, not a splintered legion where no man could trust another at his back.

Crutcher stood and searched the playa below. There was nothing but an occasional clump of greasewood and farther off some broken cottonwoods. He had expected to see nothing. Thumb had no reason to veer back toward Fort Bowie. He would be riding away from the army's strength, not into it.

But Crutcher had had another reason for climbing the ridge. He needed to be alone for a moment, to let his blood cool.

Sculls' stupid remark had stirred his anger deeply. Stirred it deeply because the emotions were still deep.

Morning Rain.

Crutcher looked out across the desert once again, then let his head rest on his drawn-up knees. That dark-eyed woman who had loved him the winter long, her life like a comforting blanket thrown over his own empty, harsh world.

Morning Rain had moved with a grace all her own—a grace peculiar to her and to wild things. As a doe moved, she moved quietly, eyes flashing, back erect. And she had loved him and presented him with a son as a gift of her love: a round-faced, dark-eyed boy with fly-away black hair and a puckered little smile which grew into a grin as Daniel grew older.

They had had six years of hunting, fishing in the quiet streams along the red-stoned Arroyo Grande and higher up on the Fugitive River of the Chocolates.

Daniel, his eager face learning all Crutcher knew, all his mother knew of the wild country, the tiny sights and colors of the desert, the grandeur of the empty land . . . six years before the cholera had taken them both.

Crutcher did not lift his head. He hid his face and wept the bitter tears he would never show another man.

Four

They strung out southward in the gray hours of morning, the horses plodding doggedly through the early haze. The flat whiteness of the salt playas gradually gave way to shallow dunes with sparse, yellow grass. Still farther to the south, toward the rails, the terrain was barren, broken at intervals by jagged flame-colored stone and jutting black basaltic chimneys.

They nooned at Riodoso Wells, the last watering spot known to the soldiers. The wells were in shade, the walls of the canyon rising high above them. The water was cold, sweet from the deep blue cisterns.

Sculls was leaning against the high slab of blue stone, his hating eyes locked on Crutcher who was rubbing his horse down.

"I'll kill him," Sculls grumbled.

"Best wait a time," Denver told him. The red-haired man was cleaning the sand from his rifle. Sculls turned toward him sharply. "We've got use for that man—Beamon wouldn't like it."

"Beamon can . . ." Sculls clamped his mouth shut, swallowing the rest of the curse.

Denver said nothing. He watched Sculls storm off, lugging his saddle. Sculls was unpredictable and didn't like being told what to do by any man, Jasper Beamon or Lieutenant Aston. Sculls made a lousy soldier because of it. Yet Sculls, like Denver, had only joined the army to escape from the past where he had enjoyed a bad reputation under a different name. Denver made up his mind to say nothing else to Sculls—he bore a grudge badly. There was mention of five men in Sculls' past who had found that out.

Still, Beamon was right—they needed Crutcher. Perhaps more than they needed the hard-headed Sculls.

Aston walked up beside Crutcher, removing his hat. He nodded and rinsed his face in the icy water, standing when he was through.

"I guess our lives are in your hands from here on, Crutcher," the lieutenant said.

"Oh?" Crutcher finished cinching his saddle, his strong hands working deftly. Then he turned, smiling, to the young officer. "Why so?"

"The water. We've no idea where to find it from here on. Hunter is a good scout, but he doesn't know the area. Besides—I guess you know Thumb's tendencies better than anyone, don't you?''

There was something of an accusation in Aston's words, but Crutcher only nodded and replied. "I reckon."

"Well, I hope the colonel's faith in you is justified, Crutcher. I don't have much confidence in you—I may as well get that out in the open.''

"I guessed as much," Crutcher said. "It's the woman—Rebecca. You've got a good case on her, don't you, Aston?''

"It's not her!" Aston flared, but from his reaction, it was obvious that was just it. "You're a divisive force here, Crutcher. A civilian and an antagonistic one. You've already tangled with my troopers. Frankly, I think you're only here for the reward money. And I wonder just how hostile you are to Thumb.''

"I'm not hostile to Thumb at all," Crutcher answered truthfully. "But he's plenty hostile toward me. Fact is, I used to get along with Thumb real well . . . after I got to understand him.'' Crutcher stopped, shutting off his memories. "But you're right about one thing, Aston—without me, you and your men will dry up and blow away out on this desert.''

"And with you?" Aston asked dryly.

"You've a chance. A small chance. If Thumb don't get us. Or those men who're tracking us.''

"What men?" Aston asked with surprise.

"I can't say. I've no idea who they are, but they've been back there since Cheer. Whoever they are, it's the gold they want, and if we do

39

somehow manage to get it back from Thumb—which ain't likely—we've got them to consider."

Aston was silent, turning back toward the north where he saw nothing, expected to see nothing. Yet Crutcher believed they were being followed and it seemed he had no reason to lie about that. Unless they were with Crutcher.

Aston let his dark eyes again study the tall, sandy-haired man in buckskin. Crutcher's eyes told nothing. His face was hard, but placid. This was the face of a man who had seen much, feared little. Was it the face of treachery? Aston could only guess.

They let the horses drink their fill, then moved southward until they came into the deep, shadowed red-stone canyon where the train lay scattered across the canyon floor.

Crutcher rode slowly into the deep cut, eyes searching the landscape, noticing the crosses sunk next to the hastily dug graves. He swung down and walked slowly back and forth, leading his pony, eyes probing the secrets the earth still held. Each tiny scar, each broken blade of dry grass revealing a part of the message held by the land.

"Twenty or so," Ivory Hunter guessed as he and Crutcher sat alone atop a low hillrise.

"They're carrying Winchesters," Crutcher added. He had gathered up a handful of brass cartridges from beyond the dunes where the Apaches had positioned themselves during the attack. He held them in his rough palm, showing them to Ivory. Then Crutcher exhaled deeply and cast them away.

"It's a fool's mission, Ivory."

"I reckon," the old man said.

"They outman us. Outgun us. They know the land."

"They surely do," Ivory agreed. The old man locked eyes with Crutcher and spat out a stream of tobacco.

"And, they're fighting men through and through," Crutcher said, stepping back into the saddle. The buckskin pony sidestepped and blew before settling down. "I'm not so sure about these men with us," Crutcher mused.

"They'll do in a pinch," Ivory said. He took off his low-crowned hat and wiped back his silky white hair. "Wren's a fighter. The Kentuckian is a dead shot . . ."

"And the rest?" Crutcher asked sourly.

"The lieutenant means well."

"That never took any scalps." Crutcher was silent a minute, the cooling breeze off the high mountains washing over them as day faded. "You know we're being followed—white men."

"I know," Ivory spat. "Aston figgers you know who they are."

Crutcher shook his head as they started back down the sandy slope. "I don't—but I mean to find out. I don't favor dogs at my heels."

Aston stood, arms akimbo, as Crutcher and Ivory came down the slope, the horses going nearly to their haunches in the deep drift sand.

"Well?" he demanded.

41

"Twenty warriors," Crutcher reported. "They rode out south, down Arroyo Colorado. I'd guess they'll have to veer west toward Zorro Wells if they need water . . . that," Crutcher said, lifting serious blue eyes to Aston, "or Descanso."

"Descanso?"

"It's a hole-in-the-wall adobe town," Ivory Hunter explained, "five miles above the border. Can't be half a hundred folks living there—half of them women and kids. If Thumb needs supplies bad, it'd be the place."

"What's your guess, Crutcher?" Aston asked coolly.

"Knowin' Thumb like I do?" Crutcher said bitterly. "I can't say, Lieutenant. I would think he'd fight shy of populated areas just now. The Mexicans might have come across the line, chasing him. They've got water at Zorro, as for food—they can scrounge that on their own. But it's anybody's guess." Crutcher raised his eyebrows slightly. "I suppose it's your decision to make, Aston."

"Sergeant?" Aston asked, turning to Wren.

"It's anybody's guess," Wren shrugged. The big man glanced at Crutcher, but he could see Crutch wasn't holding anything back.

"We can track 'em," Crutcher suggested, "but it'll be slow going, maybe impossible across the dunes. It might be too late for Descanso if we try it that way."

"It could be too late for Descanso right now, couldn't it?" Aston argued.

"Could be," Crutcher agreed.

"I guess it's up to you, sir," Wren said, his sober eyes on Aston. It was a tough decision. If Thumb was making for the Wells and the troop proceeded to Descanso, there was every chance the Chiricahua would make his escape. Yet if Thumb raided Descanso, there would be civilian casualties. Many of them.

Aston made his decision.

"We'll ride for the town, Sergeant Wren," Aston said tightly.

"Very good, sir."

Crutcher said nothing, but swung into the saddle of his buckskin, still thinking of those riders behind them and of Thumb, who undoubtedly knew the soldiers were tracking him and might take the opportunity to add a few scalps to his war lance.

They rode through the evening hours, watering briefly at a seep known to Crutcher low in the foothills which were grassy as they approached the low basin where the town of Descanso sat, nestled among low pinyon pine and scrub oak trees.

Darkness overtook them before they could sight the town, but as yet they had seen no smoke, heard no gunfire.

"Don't mean a thing," Ferguson said pessimistically. "The start they had on us, the fires could be cold, Thumb long gone."

Crutcher had to agree. They had been overriding Indian sign—unshod ponies in a group of eight or so, but it was impossible to tell

43

if they were Thumb's tracks or those of another band of Indians.

Aston was for riding through the night, but after they nearly lost Denver and Ferguson on a loose slope of shale, the weary officer finally agreed to camp. They started a low cookfire in a small park sheltered on three sides by rising red-rust cliffs and unsaddled the ponies.

Frank Aston was bone weary, his eyes raw so that they grated with each blink of his red-rimmed eyelids. He sat on a low boulder, hat beside him, drinking his third cup of coffee. His had been a brief, so far undistinguished career since coming West. He thought occasionally of that—of being isolated from channels of contact in the East.

Yet just now he thought only of the weary miles behind, the dangerous adversary ahead of him. Aston had not yet seen Indian combat and if he dwelled on it, he found a hollow fear growing in the pit of his stomach.

Was he a coward—no, he decided with fervor. Simply inexperienced. He closed his eyes for a moment, the picture of Rebecca coming into his mind—her eyes when she had been told that her son was taken. First she had lost her husband, now her son. Aston had volunteered for this mission out of gallantry; he would see it through with guts.

Standing, he walked to the fire where Ivory Hunter sat smoking a stubby pipe.

"We should have some guards posted," Aston said to the old man.

"You want me out?" Ivory asked, squinting across the fire.

"Yes. You and Crutcher . . ." It was then that it struck Aston. He hadn't seen the scout for over an hour. He was gone!

"Sergeant Wren!" Aston shouted. Wren got up, rolling his sleeves down.

"Sir?"

"Where's Crutcher?"

"He saddled up and rode out, Lieutenant. I figured you sent him . . ." Yet Wren could see from Aston's fiery expression that this was not the case. "I guess he had a reason," Wren said with weak apology.

"I guess he did, Sergeant," Aston said coldly. "And it had better be a damned good one."

Aston watched the deep canyons, seeing nothing. A lone high star peered through a veil of cloud above the canyon walls.

"It had better be damned good."

Five

Crutcher rode higher into the sharp ridged mountains. Now he found sparse timber, mostly pinyon with a scattering of stunted cedar. The night was moonless, cooler in these high reaches where the night breezes swept the heat of day away.

His horse had traveled a distance that day, so Crutcher moved slowly, picking his way across the dark canyons, along the jagged high ridges.

He had climbed so high to be downwind from them and because they would least expect a man above them in these rugged, broken hills.

Once, half an hour earlier, he had thought he saw the glimmer of a low fire, but now he could not locate it through the timber. He halted the buckskin on a narrow outcropping, but heard nothing but the creaking of the trees in the wind, the distant hooting of an owl.

Suddenly the horse's head came up and Crutcher smiled, patting the horse's neck. He worked cautiously downslope, crossing a narrow swale and then dipping into a pinyon-strewn, rocky ravine. A pebble rolled from under the buckskin's hooves and Crutcher's breath caught.

He smelled it now—the smell of a dead fire hanging in the air. He slid from the saddle, slipping his Winchester over his back, and tied the buckskin with a slipknot.

Crutcher moved on cat feet down the gravelly slope, keeping to the timber as long as possible, then darting across an open meadow some hundred yards wide until he was at the lip of an overhanging ridge. The wind was strengthening some now, singing in the timber . . . and they were square below him.

In the dim light it was a time before he could make out any faces. Then the hawk-faced man turned in profile to him and Crutcher knew him. Jasper Beamon—a buzzard in a man's boots. He was respected for his caution among his peers, despised by those who knew him well enough to recognize the soul of a grave digger in him.

Crutcher lay pressed against the cap rock, studying the camp carefully. Ten men, perhaps more if they had a lookout posted, and they had spare horses with them.

Beamon he had recognized instantly, and by searching the camp he eventually saw Reg Quailer, a bear of a man with a scent for carrion nearly as strong as Beamon's.

He could make out none of the others in this light, but Crutcher had seen enough. Beamon was hunting—hunting gold.

Crutcher slipped back from the edge of the bluff and returned to his horse, moving deliberately, carefully. He doubted they would have a man posted up here—to climb the bluff from their position would take more ambition than Beamon's whole crew possessed. Yet he had learned to take nothing for granted; and it was midnight, a quarter moon rising across the desert when he finally reached the buckskin.

So Beamon was following the troops. Why?

Crutcher rode slowly downslope, angling toward the army camp.

The answer had to be the gold. Yet how had he come to know of it? It was not general knowledge, Crutcher knew. Yet a man like Beamon had his contacts—perhaps within the army. That gave Crutcher something more to mull over.

Knowing Beamon, it would be the badman's plan to let Thumb and the troopers have at each other, then bring his own gunnies swooping in like vultures for the kill.

Crutcher slipped into camp several hours before dawn, unsaddled the buckskin, and was asleep before he had rolled up in his blanket. An hour later he was roused by a vituperative Aston.

"Crutcher!"

Crutcher opened an eye, peered at the stars

48

and rolled slowly from his bed. Aston was hovering over him, fists clenched.

"Mornin'."

"I don't know where the hell you've been, or why. I have my suspicions, however, and I don't like any of them. This is the last chance, Crutcher. I told you before that you could ride with us or ride out. This is my command," Aston said, waving a finger nearly in Crutcher's eyes. "And by God, I'll have no mavericks in it!"

At that Aston spun away, hesitated as if he would add something, and then waving an angry hand, strode to his horse.

Crutcher walked to the fire, gulped two cups of scalding coffee and stuffed his mouth full of pan bread.

Ivory Hunter, hat back on his head, smiled cautiously and asked, "Find out who they was?"

Crutcher glanced back at Aston and nodded.

"Jasper Beamon," he said, around a mouthful of bread.

"Don't you think you ought to tell the lieutenant?" Ivory asked.

"Maybe. Maybe not." Ivory frowned curiously and Crutcher went on. "Beamon's been tipped by somebody. Maybe someone in this troop. Let them think they're getting away with something. Anyway," Crutcher went on, swinging onto his pony's back, "we don't have to worry about Beamon until we've locked horns with Thumb. Maybe then we won't have a damn thing to worry about anyway," he concluded pensively.

Hunter shook his head and stuffed his cold pipe into his pocket. The long-jointed mountain man stepped into the saddle, following Crutcher from the camp.

It was three hours before they caught sight of Descanso. The adobe-walled town was set on a low mesa, affording a view of the high desert surrounding the sleepy town. White smoke rose lazily into the skies as they rounded the twist in the rough trail, catching their first glimpse of it.

Aston reined up, Wren beside him. The lieutenant cursed softly.

"Peaceful as Sunday mornin', isn't it?" Wren commented.

"Peaceful." Aston took in a deep, dismal breath. That meant that Thumb had not ridden this way, but had veered toward Zorro Wells as Crutcher had guessed.

Crutcher had reined up beside the lieutenant now and Aston shot a piercing glance at the scout.

"I guess I should have listened to you, Crutcher," Aston said with sarcasm.

"You did what seemed right," Crutcher said gently. He could see the frustration in Aston's eyes and, despite the animosity the officer seemed to feel toward Crutcher, Crutcher had nothing against Aston—the man had tried to do his duty, that was all.

"We haven't lost more than a day," Crutcher said, hooking his knee casually over the saddle horn as he spoke.

"A day," Aston repeated. "That's not much

. . . unless Thumb makes for the border. If he does that, we're out of it already."

There was nothing to be said to that, so Crutcher suggested, "We should maybe ride into Descanso—there's a chance someone may have spotted the Apaches."

"We could use fresh horses, Lieutenant," Wren put in, "if there's any to be had."

Aston pondered it a moment. By going into Descanso, the trail back to the west would be lengthened, but the riding would be easier. The jagged tumbled mountains could be skirted. Too, as Wren said, they could use fresh mounts.

"All right. Take them forward, Wren."

Descanso was asleep as they trailed its dusty red streets, or seemed to be, but these were a wary people, isolated as they were, and from time to time Crutcher saw a face peering from the window, a white-clad Mexican kid scooting down the alley with a banging of a door following.

Aston stopped beside an old man who was carrying two buckets of water on a yoke. "Pardon me—where is the office of the *alcalde?*"

"*Alcalde?*" The weathered, brown face turned to Aston and a long finger stretched out. "Cantina."

Aston stared at the saloon, wiped his forehead in frustration and repeated his question. "The *alcalde?* Your mayor's office?"

"Sí," the old man explained patiently. "The *alcalde*—his office is the cantina."

They swung down in front of the low adobe

building which had rough, barked poles protruding from the roof in front. There was shade under the awning, but it was no cooler there. A dry breeze swirled the dust of the main street and the horses stood without moving, only occasionally flicking an ear to shed a fly.

"Reckon they got beer inside?" Sculls asked Wren.

"I do." Wren stood with his arms crossed, beside the door. From within they heard the shrill laughter of a woman as Aston stamped wearily onto the porch. Sculls' eyes lighted.

"The men could use some relaxation," Sculls said to the lieutenant. Aston was in no mood for it.

"We've come out undermanned, underarmed and poorly prepared. I won't make it worse by letting this patrol turn to rabble. The liquor, Sergeant Wren, is off limits—the women doubly so. I won't risk an incident."

Sculls turned his back and hung across the hitch rail, muttering to Denver. "Treats us like dirt, don't he?"

"His day's comin'," Denver said softly, watching as Crutcher followed Aston into the cantina, the solid door closing behind them.

There were half a dozen men seated at tables, all but one town men by their looks. The other was a dust-coated vaquero. Alone at a table in one corner a dark-eyed young woman sat drinking whisky. Crutcher flashed a glance at the girl then looked back once again, harder.

"Yolanda," he said in disbelief.

"You know her?" Aston asked.

"Yeah. I know her."

"I am looking for the *alcalde*," Aston announced. They were introduced to a corpulent, mustached man who had been sipping beer, fanning himself. Now, however, he rose and put his dark coat on, striding to them.

"I am Rialto—*alcalde* of Descanso."

"Sir," Aston acknowledged. "I am Lieutenant Aston. This is Crutcher."

"I am pleased to meet you, sir," Rialto said. Then he glanced briefly at Crutcher. "Him, I know."

"I won't be staying," Crutcher said with a short smile.

"Good—furniture is difficult to obtain here, as are show bulls."

Crutcher smiled to himself and Aston shot him a worried glance.

"Do not worry, Lieutenant," Rialto said, offering him a chair. "I do not hold grudges. Perhaps it is healthy for a man my age to walk fifteen miles across the desert at night in only his—pardon me—long johns, in the dead of winter."

Aston glanced painfully at Crutcher who smiled despite himself. Aston decided he had brought the wrong man in with him and plunged quickly into his business.

"We require two things, sir. Horses and any reports you may have heard of the presence of the Chiricahua known as Thumb."

"Thumb." Rialto's black eyes went hard and

he shook his head somberly. "The man is an animal, no?" He looked up at Crutcher as he asked that. "Isolated as we are, we fear his savages greatly. Believe me, you will have fresh horses, sir. He must be hunted down. Tell me— where is the main body of your men now located?"

Aston had to tell him directly, "This is my force, sir."

Rialto's face was frozen in incomprehension, then suddenly he laughed. "I see you have a sense of humor." But Aston's face cooled this flare-up of humor. Rialto spread his hands, looking from Crutcher to Aston. "But this is absurd!"

"We will require horses," Aston said evenly.

"Of course. As for rumors of Thumb's location—I have heard many rumors. But none of them have more weight than the next. He is a ghost on the desert . . . until he decides to roost."

Rialto sighed again, heavily, and raised his bulk from the chair with some difficulty. "Armando!" he cried to a smallish man who was dozing in the corner. "Let us look at your horses!"

Rialto picked up his hat, formed it slightly and planted it at a rake on his glossy hair. With a short arm briefly around Aston's shoulder, he turned with the officer toward the door.

Crutcher had remained behind. He looked at the far table where the girl sat, her face covered with her hands, her long black hair falling

54

across her face. She wore black with a splash of a red sash around her waist. She did not move as Crutcher strode silently across the floor.

"Yolanda?"

He stood a moment looking at her, but she did not answer and he pulled out a chair, turning it, sitting astride, his hat placed on the table. The whisky bottle was half empty.

"Yolanda," he repeated softly, a hand stretching out to touch a strand of that raven hair.

"Go away, señor," she said, her voice muffled behind her hands. "Not today. Not today."

"Yolanda," Crutcher said gently, and some hint of recognition stirred in the girl's mind. Slowly she spread her hands and she stared. Just stared at Crutcher for a long minute, her black eyes stained red by the liquor.

Then she burst into a harsh, crackling laugh.

"You!" she shrieked. "You—Crutcher!" she laughed again, wildly, her shoulders trembling. Then she stopped, tears rolling down her faded cheeks, and still her shoulders trembled, but it was with racking sobs. She buried her face in her hands once more.

"Go away, Crutcher. Go away!"

"I will. After a time."

"You . . ." Yolanda began furiously, her fiery eyes slashing at Crutcher, her head proudly held high. Then she took a deep breath, her breast rising gently, and she patted her bodice for a handkerchief which she found. She dabbed at her eyes, smiling weakly.

"I am so surprised to see you . . ." she said.

55

Her hand went automatically to the bottle and Crutcher watched as she poured a deep drink which she took in a swallow.

"So—" Yolanda sniffed, again attempting a smile. "How has it gone?"

"All right." Crutcher smiled briefly, a terse smile which turned the corners of his generous mouth up for a brief moment as if they had been yanked up, then as quickly released. His blue eyes were sober, veiled. "Do you mind?" he asked. Yolanda nodded and Crutcher reached out, filled her glass with liquor and drank it down himself.

"You are here," Yolanda began, her voice catching "with Morning Rain . . . ?"

"Morning Rain is dead. Daniel is dead," Crutcher said without looking at the woman.

"I did not . . ."

"Let's get out of this place," Crutcher said, cutting off an awkward apology.

Yolanda nodded and followed Crutcher to the side door which he opened, letting the telling white light cut across her face which was sallow, prematurely lined. He noticed now that her always ample body had filled out even more, and that she walked with a weariness which belongs only to those who have no place to walk, no reason to attempt it.

They moved up the hillrise behind the cantina—a barren yellow hill studded with gray boulders and patches of nopal cactus. Crutcher noticed only then that he was holding the woman's hand. Yolanda seemed relieved when he dropped it suddenly.

There was a goat path which wound to a shelf of rock a hundred feet up on the small hill, and from there the small town of Descanso shrunk to a miniature; yet the vast and yellow-white desert seemed only larger, a blue haze obscuring the distant horizon.

A dry breeze wafted up the canyon, lifting Yolanda's skirts which she held down with her hands between her knees as they sat on the ledge. She said nothing and Crutcher was silent as well, taking the whisky bottle to his lips until it was drained.

She had been a fine looking woman, and was yet—with a straight nose, high cheekbones, slashing black eyes and a voluptuous figure. Yet now something had dried up within her, a part of her soul had withered as the dead branch of a flourishing tree. It was in her eyes and in her face.

"Whatever happened to us, Crutcher?" she said finally. "Whatever happened to our lives?"

"Nothing happened, Yolanda," Crutcher said with a whisky smile. "Why, we're still here!"

"Are we?" she mused. Then she turned her softened eyes to him and he had to turn his gaze down. "Why are you here?" she asked suddenly.

"Helpin' those fool army boys hunt Thumb," he answered after a moment's silence.

"And then—if you should catch him?"

"I reckon he'll kill us all," Crutcher said.

Yolanda looked closely now at Crutcher. A

57

fine, proud man with sandy hair, a small scar on his left cheek, blue-gray eyes which had seen war and hard weather, tasted love and, despite their hardness, flashed with humor and grew soft when the time for softness was there—this she knew, for she had known their softness, their love.

"Thumb—always Thumb. Still Thumb . . . interminably," she said.

"It seems so, don't it," Crutcher admitted.

"But why do you do it, Crutcher?" Yolanda asked, suddenly animated, as if withdrawing from her dry cocoon. "Chase Thumb?"

"There's money in it . . ." Crutcher said, but she knew him too well and there was no sense sketching the rest of the lie.

"A woman?" Yolanda asked, eyes downward.

"There's a woman. A lady," Crutcher said, keeping his eyes on the desert where an answer lay. "Nice lady—Thumb has her boy."

Yolanda seemed not to hear him. She glanced at the empty bottle wistfully.

"I know," she said. The wind was in her long hair, twisting it into profuse arabesques.

"You know?" Crutcher repeated. A long-eared jack rabbit loped across the vaguely green flats below, and the breeze, which was dry and choking yet, had stilled somewhat. Yolanda turned to him, her lip tremulous.

"I know where Thumb is."

Six

Crutcher said nothing for a long moment. Yolanda's dark eyes locked with his briefly; then she turned her head away, biting her lip as if she wished to recall her words.

"You know where Thumb is?" Crutcher asked, genuinely astonished.

"I know," she said in a small voice. "Yaqui Bob told me that he saw them ride through three days ago. He hid in the rocks and watched as they took his horses. He told me, me alone . . ." Yolanda smiled ironically. "I believe he thinks I loved Thumb."

"But did Bob say where Thumb was heading?" Crutcher wanted to know. Yolanda stared at him.

"You know Yaqui Bob," she shrugged. "Besides—why mention it? I don't want you to chase him, Crutcher."

Her hand stretched out to his and he twitched with impatience.

"I've hired on to do it, Yolanda."

"Yes—and so you will do it, if it is your death." Her eyes flashed briefly with that old fire as she spat these words out with disgust. "Why do you wish to die, Crutcher? You are as mad as Thumb."

"Yolanda, I . . ."

"Sh!" Her hand went gently to his mouth. "Don't speak of Thumb. Don't speak of dying. Do you remember when you met me, Crutcher?" she laughed. "A poor wren, no?"

"I remember."

"I was a prim Spanish girl before Thumb took me—you should have known me. I strutted through my father's gardens, proud as a peahen. Beautiful—they all said I was so beautiful, Crutcher."

He nodded, smiling vaguely.

"Then this savage, deep-chested man . . . this Thumb dragged me off my horse and took me to his camp." Yolanda was silent a while, perhaps recalling that young girl's terror.

"He took me for his woman," Yolanda said, watching the distances wistfully. "And I hated him—if I could have found a knife, I would have driven it into his black heart that first night! Into my own . . . Morning Rain was my only friend in that savage camp."

Yolanda had kept Crutcher's hand in her own. Now she turned it over, examining the rough creases, the hard callus.

"I remember the first morning I saw you. You were with Morning Rain. I had to peer through the tent flap. Thumb would have beaten me if I came out—the whites would have known he had me.

"But you were young and strong, lean. You had a black horse then, remember?"

"I do," Crutcher said, himself becoming lost in the memory of those days when Thumb had been a friend . . . when Morning Rain had been his.

"You two splashed in the river, playing love games . . . and I longed for you to see me, Crutcher, to rescue me. She spoke of you often, and I grew jealous . . . especially when Thumb came to me."

Yolanda smiled weakly, dropped Crutcher's hand and stood, the wind pressing her dress to her thighs.

"And later . . . when I did know you," she went on, "I could not ask you to take me away for fear Thumb would kill you."

"So long ago," Crutcher said, standing as well. "But you found your freedom that summer when the soldiers came after Thumb."

"Freedom!" she laughed. And her laughter was so harsh, so bitter that Crutcher had to look away.

"Do you know what that freedom has meant? Do you know what it means to have been an Apache's woman? My father would not look at my face. I discovered—painfully, slowly—that I was good for only one sort of life after that."

"I didn't know, Yolanda. I'm sorry," Crutcher said, and he meant it deeply. He could imagine how things had gone for her.

"No—but it was none of your fault. I am sorry for your sorrow, Crutcher; you are sorry for mine. That is the way of this life."

Yolanda started down the path toward Descanso. Far below Crutcher could see the troopers scattered out across town, perhaps looking for him.

"But Thumb," he said, grabbing her by the shoulders as they reached a bend in the path. "I must know where he is."

"No." Yolanda's dark eyes sunk into thoughtfulness. "Unless I could . . ." she grabbed Crutcher's arm tightly, tearing at his sleeve. "I want out of here! Out of Descanso," she said breathlessly. "I could take you. You could let me ride with you . . . as far as Conejo at least!"

"Conejo—then he's ridden west," Crutcher said.

"I did not say that, Crutcher!" she said frantically. "I loved you! Can't you do this for me? This much?"

"No." He shook his head slowly.

"Then I won't tell you what I know."

"I guess we'll have to find him ourselves then." Crutcher's eyes were implacable. "He's riding from Yaqui Bob's toward Conejo—I'll find his tracks, hard rock or drift sand."

Crutcher turned away from Yolanda, but he couldn't tear his arm free. He turned back, and their eyes met. She pressed her body to him and she kissed him hotly, the salt of tears running into their mouths from Yolanda's deep black eyes.

"Crutcher . . ." she breathed.

"I won't have you hurt!" he said sharply, pushing her to arm's length.

"I am hurt now," she said, her voice subdued. Her breast heaved with barely controlled passions. "Thumb!" she laughed recklessly. "He would not hurt me."

"Maybe not. But maybe he's got warriors with him who wouldn't know your scalp from mine. At a distance a rifleman can't tell much."

"You'd have me live on here . . . as I have? Withering away. In Conejo, at least I could buy a train ticket. I deserve a new life too, Crutcher," she said. Her eyes were pleading. Crutcher heard the voices below now, calling his name.

"You do. But you deserve to plain *live*, Yolanda. Now is not the time to ride that desert. You should know it."

"Crutcher!"

He turned back one last time and kissed her full mouth, surprising her no more than himself. Then he squeezed her shoulder with his rough hand and walked down the long slope, the sound of the troopers calling to him growing louder, more angry as he neared Descanso.

"What's the fuss?" Crutcher asked, sidling up to where Wren, fists on his hips stood near the horses.

"The fuss!" Wren laughed angrily. "Crutch, the boys have been looking for you for an hour. Aston's ready to pull out—he's fuming at the ears." Wren glanced around him cautiously, then seriously asked Crutcher, "Why don't you just drop out Crutch? Just let it go. Hell, man, you know as well as I do that all you're doing by finding water for them is keeping them alive long enough to die under Thumb's lance."

"I know it." Crutcher was throwing his saddle on the leggy roan they had gotten for him. He looked across the horse's back at Wren. "But there's a kid out there, Wren. A six year old boy . . . Daniel was just six," he said, his voice lowered.

"Damnit, Crutch, you got guts, but not a whole lot of brains," the big sergeant said, slapping the roan's rump. There was something else on Wren's mind, but he fell silent as Sculls and Denver came nearer.

The troopers stayed at a distance, lounging in the shadows.

"He gets all the privileges, don't he," Sculls said, a smoke drooping from the corner of his mouth. His long, dark face, darkened further yet by the black stubble of beard, was glowering.

"He was up there drinkin' whisky with a woman—White seen 'em come down," Sculls went on in response to the red-headed man's unasked question.

"You don't seem all that mad," Denver said slowly. Denver was weighing every word to Sculls now; the man was growing unbalanced out here. Beamon would have to take care of Sculls.

"Hell!" Sculls laughed. "Let him have his whisky now . . . I'll be drinking good rye, with a lady on my lap, when Crutcher has rotted to the worms. That's a promise, too," Sculls said, those black eyes going utterly cold so that Denver had to shudder a little under their ferocious gaze. Jasper Beamon would have to do something about Sculls, eventually. Denver would see to it. He was on a hair trigger.

Corporal White, his dirty hat low over his eyes, stepped up on the walk beside his two cronies.

"Watch this," he said gleefully. "Aston's comin'."

White crossed his arms and, grinning, leaned against the adobe wall of the cantina, watching a sunburned, furious Aston ride to where Wren and Crutcher were waiting.

Aston swung from his pony while it was still moving and in three running steps he was to Crutcher. He swung the tall, buckskinned man around by the shoulder and, with all of his might, threw a right fist against Crutcher's lean jaw.

"Lieutenant!" Wren shouted, scrambling under the roan's belly to grab the officer.

"Let me go, Wren!"

Crutcher stood there without moving, blood

65

trickling from the corner of his mouth, his blue eyes calm.

"Let me go!"

"No, sir!" Wren wrestled him away as Crutcher stood watching. Ivory Hunter, Benton and Ferguson, the Kentuckian, had just ridden up from searching south of town and they managed to get their horses between Aston and Crutcher who was cinching his saddle.

"Sir, you can't lose control of yourself like this," Wren insisted, his bear arms still holding the struggling Aston.

"You're a friend of his!"

"Yes, sir. And I'm your NCO. It ain't seemly—not in front of the troops."

Aston nodded, took a deep breath and stopped struggling. As Wren let go, he retrieved his hat and dusted it off, still glaring at Crutcher.

"That man . . . !" Aston muttered.

"Sir—we still need him," Wren reminded him.

"Yes. I suppose so. But when we get back to Bowie . . ." Aston let his threat fall to silence. That leering Sculls was on the porch watching him. Wren was right—the men had no business seeing this.

It was hot, Aston was tired. His legs were wooden from the days in the saddle. He knew, better than any of them, the futility of this mission.

"I just lost my temper," Aston stated. "But," he said, remembering, his face brightening, "something good's come out of Descanso. I found someone not five minutes ago who knows where Thumb is."

Wren blinked curiously. Aston went on.

"He's heading for a place called Conejo—the girl will show us exactly where."

"A girl!" Wren said, startled.

"Yes. All she wants is an escort as far as Conejo and she'll guide us to Thumb's sign."

"Sir . . ." Wren stammered. "With these men . . . out there? We don't need no woman."

"Wren—we need her! We need to find Thumb and this Yolanda knows where he is."

"So did I," Crutcher said quietly. His eyes were in the shade of his hat. There was still blood trickling from his mouth as he faced Aston. "She told me an hour ago—but I didn't make her no promise to take her to Conejo."

Crutcher nodded, led the roan to the rusted iron watering trough, leaving Aston to stare blankly at Wren.

"She already told Crutcher . . . that's where he was," Aston mumbled.

"It appears," Wren said thoughtfully.

"Damn! Now I have done it." From up the street they could see Yolanda riding toward them, a carpetbag tied behind the saddle of her gray-tailed white horse. "And I thought my luck was running right, Wren."

"Sir," Wren said, spitting on the ground, "I'd say your luck wasn't all that bad."

Aston frowned and watched as Wren swung heavily into the saddle.

"I don't get you, Sergeant."

"Way I look at it, sir, you're shot full of luck. You're damned lucky Crutcher didn't tear your arm off and beat you over the head with it back there."

Seven

The land spread out in a vast yellow-gold tableau below them. On the low hills where they sat there was a dusting of gray grass, here and there the shade of an oak or sycamore, but below, to the south and west, all of the land was barren, twisted into a portrait of hell.

Reddish mesas rose up, broke off and crumbled away. Great fields of calderas—dead volcanoes—littered the sterile landscape where only the scorpion, the rattlesnake, the cholla cactus lived. All of life was barbed and hard-shelled on that endless desert, as were the men who lived upon it. The Chiricahua.

"Thumb's come home," Crutcher said.

"How could any people live out there?" Aston said with wonder. His pale face was streaked with perspiration, blotchy with red dust.

"They had no choice," Crutcher answered. "They were pushed onto it. Not only by the whites," he went on. "The Apache have always been a warring, far-ranging nation. I don't expect there's a tribe between here and the Canadian border Thumb or his ancestors haven't warred with."

"Canada?" Wren said with surprise.

"That's what Thumb tells me," Crutcher said, turning to the big man. "Says that his people first came out of the far north and stormed their way southward. A fighting people, I guess their blood is running out . . . so they have come to this place."

"Where's Yaqui Bob's?" Aston demanded.

"Not far," Yolanda said. She was holding up remarkably well, considering the amount of time she had spent out of doors recently. She lifted a finger and showed Aston where the Arroyo Seco intersected the Tortuga at the base of the gray, amputated hills called the Dedos.

"His shack is there, where the water basin is. In winter—if it rains—the water from the Tortuga rushes into Arroyo Seco and fills his catch basins under ground. Then there is water for his sheep."

"There's water there now?" Aston wanted to know. Water was their prime concern now— and it was in their thoughts constantly.

"Sí. There should be water there. That is why Thumb went to Yaqui Bob's, I think."

"And Conejo, Yolanda?" Aston wanted to know. "Where is that?"

Again she pointed and Aston's eyes strained, following the direction of her finger across the vast white wasteland, through broken, treacherous canyons to the far west where an obscuring bluish haze blocked farther vision. Aston cursed under his breath and nudged his pony forward.

Yaqui Bob's was shaded by the distant hills when they reached the gray, weathered collection of shacks in late afternoon.

"Yaqui!" Crutcher called, but there was no answer. There was a slight breeze, cooling after the dry day. It lifted Yolanda's dark hair, squeaked in the shacks which were made of plastered-up ocotillo spines.

"Yaqui!"

"He may have driven his sheep into the high country," Yolanda guessed.

"Let's find those catch basins and water up the stock," Aston suggested. "It's too late to ride any farther today."

Ivory Hunter rode with Crutcher as they circled the narrow, barren valley in the deepening shadows.

"Something's wrong," the old scout said. He carried his rifle across his saddle bows, eyes squinting, searching the criss-crossing shadows.

"You're right," Crutcher agreed.

There was fresh sheep sign all around the place, hoofprints not two days old. It was doubtful Yaqui Bob had driven his sheep upcountry. If so, they should have been able to catch a glimpse of him from the hills.

71

"Look." Ivory halted and nodded toward a mule which stood tethered in a clumb of thorny mesquite. Together they rode to it and untied the animal which was biting mad at having been left standing.

"It's Bob's," Crutcher said, touching the brand. He exchanged glances with Ivory Hunter who could feel the hairs standing up on the back of his neck. There was a damp spot on the animal's saddle and Crutcher touched it to his tongue.

"Blood."

There was a tangle of sign on the ground, but in the fading light neither man could read it well, except to know that there had been a struggle in the soft sand.

Aston, Wren and Sculls were some fifty yards behind Crutcher and he turned now and raised a hand in the signal of caution. Then he and Ivory nudged their horses forward up the rocky wash toward the catch basins.

The path, winding through a patch of nopal and up onto a gray rock bench, was dark with shadow, but there was enough light to see what had happened as Crutcher crested the lip of the basin.

"Damn." Crutcher sat his horse, shaking his head bitterly. Ivory Hunter moved up beside him and the old man was shaken up some.

"They came back."

Yaqui Bob was floating in the black water of the basin, face down, his head nudging the rock wall. He was dead, cut to ribbons as were the fifty sheep which shared the death pool with him, their throats slashed.

Crutcher turned away and they met Aston coming up.

"There's no water," Crutcher said.

"But, Yolanda said . . ."

"Yaqui Bob's dead. They threw him in the water. Along with some sheep. Either Thumb came back or some of his party is trailing off in a rear guard. Whichever, it don't matter anymore to Yaqui."

They camped in a scooped-out hollow a hundred feet up on the Dedos. It was a clear, starry night and the low fire glowed red, casting flickering shadows across their faces.

"Ma'am?"

Yolanda glanced up to see the tall Kentuckian standing over her, a cup of black coffee in his hand. She smiled at his boyish manner and took the cup gratefully.

"Sorry we don't have no tea or sugar," Ferguson said.

"This will be fine," Yolanda replied. She clutched the army blanket around her shoulders and sipped from the blue enamel cup.

"Mister Crutcher?"

Crutch looked up and saw Ferguson standing there with two cups of coffee.

"Figured you might want some and I hadn't seen you around the fire," the trooper said.

"Thanks. Have a seat," Crutcher offered and with a grin, Ferguson squatted on the rock-strewn earth, watching the smoke from the fire curl into the cold skies.

"It's funny, ain't it?" Ferguson said. He had his hat tipped back, his rifle in the crook of his arm as he drank from his cup.

"Funny?" Crutcher said, studying the freckled kid's face.

"I never imagined no war like this . . . if that's what it is. We ain't fired a shot. Hell—I ain't even seen the enemy. It don't even seem that there's nobody like Thumb out there. Peaceful and empty like it is . . ."

"Until this evening?"

"Yes, sir. Until this evening. It wakes a man up."

"Stay awake, Ferguson," Crutcher said, tossing out the last of his coffee, "and you'll be fine. Just don't forget that he is out there."

The fire was burning lower. Ferguson finished his coffee as well, standing. He hesitated, then said, "She's a nice woman, ain't she? I talked with her a time as we rode today."

"She is a nice woman," Crutcher answered.

"Makes a man wonder—why'd she come out on this desert?"

"She wants to make a train connection at Conejo," Crutcher said. He had rolled up and now lay on his back, hat tilted over his eyes.

"Sir—I don't know you all that well, Mister Crutcher. But for a man who reads sign like you, I don't think you're readin' this right."

"No?" Crutcher muttered sleepily from behind his hat.

"No, sir. I mean—I seen the way her eyes

74

watch your back while she rides, the moisture that comes into 'em. She ain't ridin' for no train, sir. She's ridin' to be near you, Mister Crutcher . . . if a man asked my opinion.''

"I didn't ask," Crutcher said roughly.

"No, sir. No, sir, you didn't."

Crutcher listened to the kid's bootheels crunching gravel as he moved away across the clearing. Then he lay awake for a long time until the camp was silent, an uneasiness in him.

He rolled out early. The fire was still cold, the men rolled up but for Ivory Hunter who was taking his watch turn.

Crutcher walked his roan out and let it graze on the only patch of grass visible for a mile. Then he rubbed it down, checking its shoes and giving it water from his canteen poured into his hat.

"You take care of a horse."

"My life depends on that animal," Crutcher said, not turning back to the voice which belonged to Frank Aston.

"We haven't even begun this ride, have we, Crutcher?" Aston asked, moving around to face him. Crutcher glanced up at the young officer. He had his dark hair slicked back with water and he had a fresh shave. His uniform was as clean as possible. Crutcher picked a small stone from the horse's left foreleg hoof with his bowie and shook his head.

"No, we haven't."

Aston nodded. His young face was creased with concern as he stood, hands behind his back, watching the far distance.

"This trick with the water—poisoning it with the bodies of sheep . . . we're likely to find that from now on?"

"Likely. Thumb knows we're following. What water holes they don't naturally dry up by their own use they'll try to foul, fill in or block off. I would say it'll be damned rugged from here on, Aston."

"Can we make it?"

"It's nip and tuck," Crutcher answered.

"Damnit, man!" Aston shouted, turning with exasperation. Then he touched his forehead nervously. "I mean—can we make it?"

"Not likely," Crutcher said plainly.

"Do you think we should turn back?" Aston asked.

"Sir, that's your decision, only yours." Crutcher added. "Myself—I'm going on."

"Alone?"

"If I have to. Might stand a better chance anyway."

"Is it Rebecca?" Aston asked in a faltering voice. "Are you doing it for her?"

"Yes. Aren't you?"

Aston nodded as if slowly realizing his worst fears. Crutcher said nothing else. Let the man think what he wanted. Aston saw the boy Thumb had kidnapped as a future son, that was obvious. Crutcher perhaps saw him as a son he had once had—a boy alone.

"I figure," Crutcher said quickly, "to circle north into the Royal Gorge area. There's water

76

in those parts and Thumb likely will be heading due west. If we follow him direct, we'll hit bad water for a hundred miles."

"Won't we lose him?"

"There's a chance."

"And the woman—we'll be taking her away from Conejo, not toward it."

"That's the worst part of it, Aston; but it weren't me invited her along," Crutcher said, stepping into the saddle of his roan.

He rode slowly away as if nothing in the world was bothering him, but it disturbed him deeply that Yolanda would be riding with them if Aston decided to carry on. Crutcher had a fleeting notion to go on alone, now, before Aston had even time to make up his mind. That way Yolanda would be forced to turn back with them toward Descanso . . .

It was then that Yolanda's scream pierced the still morning air and Crutcher laid the spurs to the roan.

Eight

The horse plunged down the short slope and dug up the gravel-strewn path with Crutcher whipping it with his hat. Yolanda screamed again and Crutcher vaulted the roan through the camp in two leaps. The men were rolling out, snatching up weapons.

The screams had come from higher up, along a rocky wash near the only living things on that side of the hills, a stand of twisted manzanita.

Then he spotted her, standing half undressed behind the screen of manzanita, her hand to her mouth.

"Up there," she said, and at that moment a shot rang down the long arroyo.

Glancing quickly back, Crutcher could see the others rushing toward him, Aston in the lead, but he didn't wait for them. He kneed the roan and it climbed the twisted game trail on the barren face of the hill, hoofs clambering for footholds as Crutcher, rifle unlimbered, drove the pony upward.

Fifty feet from the peak, he swung down and let the horse go on alone, taking to the rocks himself at a low, crouching run.

Ivory Hunter's mule was picketed among some nopal and the animal's wide-eyed head came up to meet Crutcher's approach.

From the corner of his eye, he saw Ivory's body lying still on the earth and then, directly in front of him, a savagely painted face appeared above a yellowish boulder.

Crutcher brought his rifle to his shoulder and dropped to his knee, the Winchester exploding, the echoing peals rolling down the canyons.

He slid to one side, crawled behind a clump of scattered boulders and waited, eyes squinting into the sun. There was no sound, no movement.

From where he sat he could see Ivory Hunter, rifle still in his hand, blood staining the back of his nearly white, bleached buckskins.

Behind and below him, the troopers were scrambling up the trail. Afoot except for Aston who rode his black gelding barebacked, they were still a hundred yards off.

Taking in a deep breath, Crutcher scrambled up from the boulders, knocking a knee painfully. He rolled over the stones and dipped into a briefly shadowed vale, his heart pounding in his throat as he moved upward.

"Crutcher!" Aston bellowed from below. "Crutcher!"

Crutcher came around the shady side of the huge boulder and stopped, letting his rifle dangle. The Apache was lying face down on the earth, blood smearing his head and shoulders. That first, off-hand shot had taken him.

There was the clatter of horse's hoofs on the rock behind him and Crutcher swung back, his rifle cocked.

"Hold it!" Aston shouted.

Slowly Crutcher lowered the rifle and turned back to the dead Chiricahua. Ferguson, his face beet red, appeared over the boulder and he slid down to join them.

"Dead?" Aston asked.

"He is." Crutcher rolled him over. "He was bad hurt." The brave's leg was puffed and discolored with the ugly sign of gangrene. "Apparently they left him behind because of it. He was holed up here—Ivory just happened on him."

"How is Ivory?" Aston demanded.

"Wren's seein' to him," Ferguson said. "He's breathin', but losin' blood."

Ferguson slid back down the rock, rifle held high. Wren had slit Ivory Hunter's buckskin jacket open and was working on the arrow.

"Are there more of them in these rocks, Crutcher?" Aston wanted to know.

"I'd only be guessin'," Crutcher said. "But I wouldn't say it was a good place for us to stay around."

"We'll move out—if Hunter can travel."

"Sir." Crutcher locked eyes with the young officer, and told him, "We'd better be movin' whether Ivory can go or not."

"You'd leave him?" Aston asked incredulously.

"Yes, sir. Same as I'd want Ivory to leave me. Why risk the men, Yolanda, the mission for a single man. Like you say, there could well be a dozen wounded men Thumb's left behind hidden in those rocks. And if they start smelling food, looking at our horses, they'll sure as hell come down."

Aston said nothing, watching as Crutcher stepped into the saddle of his roan, his recovered hat pulled low. Each time he figured he had Crutcher categorized, the man did something to confound him.

Yolanda was huddled against the brush, sitting on a flat rock, clothes held in front of her. The man called Sculls had crept over to where she sat and she cringed each time she looked at the man's weasel eyes.

She had been taking a sponge bath when she heard a grunt, looked up to see Ivory Hunter swing around with an arrow in his chest, then watched as Hunter fired a reckless shot at the rocks, trying to hit the dusty, paint-daubed figure which dragged itself into them.

"You're a fine lookin' thing, ain't you?" Sculls asked. He stepped closer yet, his eyes glassy, a smoke dangling cold from his protruding lips. She had seen his kind.

"Go on, finish your dressing," Sculls drawled with a sharp laugh. Then his head spun back and he saw the long-geared man in buckskins sitting the roan.

"Get the hell out of here, Sculls," Crutcher said. He had the Winchester in his hands and Sculls measured the man, wondering if he would dare use it.

Discretion moved Sculls to tip his hat and turn back toward the camp, saying over his shoulder in a voice audible only to Crutcher, "You act like she's your woman—like every damned thing belongs to you. Don't forget me, Crutcher. Because I'll be comin' for you sooner or later, no matter what happens.

"And," Sculls added viciously, "I'll be comin' for that woman."

"You can't take me," Crutcher said, "not you and all of Beamon's men."

Sculls froze at those words, glanced back at Crutcher and chuckled.

"I'll be damned. You ain't quite as dumb as you look, Crutcher." Then the man swaggered off down the canyon, Yolanda staring after him, her lip trembling.

"Crutch!"

She threw herself into his arms, her heart pounding against his, and Crutcher held her stiffly for a moment, uneasy with this sign of affection.

"Finish dressing."

"Ivory—is he all right?" Yolanda asked, stepping back.

"I don't know. He's alive."

Yolanda slipped into her chemise and buttoned her white blouse over it, Crutcher looking away, sitting on a rock, holding his horse's reins until she was finished. Then they walked into camp together.

Aston had his men gathering their gear together. Sculls stood to one side with Denver and White. Ivory Hunter was near the fire, a blanket thrown over him. His eyes were distant, pale as he squinted at Crutcher who was kneeling beside him, leaning on his rifle.

"Damned careless of me, wasn't it?" the old man asked.

"I'd say so," Crutcher said, and Hunter smiled faintly.

"Aston leaving me?" Hunter asked. He twitched with pain, his facial muscles taut, then relaxing.

"I'm trying to talk him into it," Crutcher said honestly.

Ivory Hunter had traveled too many trails not to understand this. It was the way it was. An army moved too slowly with the wounded; as Thumb had understood. Too, moving at a pace required by the army meant certain death for those who might survive if left to rest.

"What do you reckon he'll do?" Ivory asked. His white hair was spread out across the ground, bits of brush woven into its silky fibers.

"I reckon he'll act like a damn fool and try and tote you," Crutcher guessed.

Ivory Hunter smiled briefly, then closed his

83

eyes, unconsciousness shutting out any cares.

"Well?" Aston was hovering over them and Crutcher, still on one knee, swiveled his head to answer the lieutenant.

"He'd best be left . . . or taken back to Descanso."

"That would cost us a man," Aston said.

"To take Ivory with us might cost us all our men," Crutcher reminded him.

"I'll have the men rig up a litter," Aston said. Crutcher shook his head, saying nothing. He walked to where Yolanda sat her white horse. She looked at him with concern.

"Will he be all right?" she asked.

"Not if Aston has his way."

"What does that mean?"

Crutcher told her about Aston's intentions and about Ivory's chances on that travois. "He'll be dragged and jolted over a hundred miles of hell, only to be helpless in the event of an attack, suffering all the time."

"There's only one person can help him . . . you, Yolanda."

"Me?" she asked, shocked by his statement.

"You could take him back, moving slowly. You'd be going away from Thumb, so you shouldn't have any trouble. Ivory could be in a bed in Descanso, resting proper in a day and a night. And, I'd feel better about you," Crutcher said, glancing toward Sculls.

"He doesn't bother me," Yolanda said, tossing her head. "And I can't go back—not there. To the way I was living . . . no!" she

84

shook her head vigorously.

"We're not going to Conejo now, Yolanda, don't you see? It doesn't make any sense for you to ride with us any longer—and you'd likely be saving Ivory's life."

"No—" she turned away, shaking her head, arms wrapped around her. Crutcher grabbed her angrily by the shoulder.

"Use your mind!" he said angrily. "Out there Ivory will die. You'll die. In Descanso you'll live."

"I don't want to live that way!" she screamed.

"And just who the hell says you have to?" Crutcher asked softly, rubbing her arm where he had grabbed it. "Who says you have to do that?"

"What else . . . ?"

"Anything else, Yolanda. Anything at all. Look, I'll talk to Aston. Ivory's under army contract—the army will pay you something for nursing him while he mends. After that— maybe you could ride back to Bowie with Ivory. Find work in Cheer . . . hell, I don't know!" He cooled his exasperation, took a deep breath and went on. "I don't want anything happening to you out there."

"You mean that, don't you?" she asked, looking searchingly into his deep blue eyes. Beneath that brittle gleam she knew so well, there was a softness visible for a fragment of a moment.

"All right," she said with a quick smile, turning her eyes down. "I will do what you say, Crutcher."

85

Crutcher walked to where Aston's men were gently lifting the old scout onto the travois behind his mule. "The girl will take him back to Descanso," Crutcher said without stopping. He walked to his roan and swung into the saddle, riding out a ways down the trail they would follow toward the Royal Gorge area.

Aston stood looking after him, hands on hips. Turning, he found Yolanda on her white horse, a single tear running across her dark cheek.

"You'll take him?" Aston asked uncertainly.

"Sí!" She spat the word out and, without an answer, she took up the reins to Ivory's mule and led the wounded man, on the travois, down the slope toward Yaqui Bob's and Descanso.

"I'll be damned," Wren muttered. "Hit the leather, men!"

They swung into line and Sculls muttered to Denver beside him, "I hate to see that get away. One of these nights I meant to pay a visit to that little . . ." The distinctive sound of a rifle being cocked just behind Sculls cut his words short. He spun to see Ferguson's rifle on him.

"Shut your mouth, Sculls," the Kentuckian said angrily.

"Sure. Sure, kid. But you've just nailed your own coffin shut. You'll never make it back from this ride."

Then the dark-faced man spat on the ground and laughed, kneeing his horse forward. Wren, off to one side, had seen the episode and he frowned heavily.

The burly sergeant had fought his share of

bloody battles and ridden the badman's trail in hard country, but this mission had a smell to it.

Sculls and his crew were up to something—the gold likely. Aston acted like he was trying to prove his manhood out on this godforsaken desert, leaving Wren with only Benton and Ferguson, and them both green.

There was Crutcher—Wren smiled to himself as he nudged his horse forward—there was always Crutch. But Crutch was Crutch, and a man never knew what to expect of him, save knowing he would side you in a fight. Maybe that was enough . . . Wren trailed the company out of Yaqui Bob's.

Nine

The land which had been hard, grew harder. They rode the endless chain of gray rock hills into the barren Royal Gorge, the only sounds the whispered curses of men, the laboring of the horses.

Here and there life sprung up, but it was harsh, seemingly useless life—a deadly gila monster squatting on a rock, panting breath into its swollen body, jewel-like eyes watching the procession of passing men.

Barrel cactus had lamed one horse already, and they picked their way carefully across the razor-edged black, volcanic stones. The men were beaten to stupors, their minds filled only with dreams of water, of coolness. The fierce sun cut at eyes, wrung perspiration from already dehydrated bodies, glittered off the mica-flecked stone, the fields of sand.

The enemy had become all of nature, the burning stone beneath the horses' hoofs, the sidewinder crawling into the bedding at night, the deadly scorpion in a boot . . . they did not think of Thumb, of destination or gold, but of an ending to this. Yet there was no end. The land bled out forever across all time.

It was a dangerous lethargy and Crutcher pinched himself mentally to avoid falling into it.

"Down there?" Aston asked through cracked, bleeding lips, and Crutcher nodded, saving the breath he would have to expend to answer.

There should have been water at Jacumba Springs. But there wasn't and Crutcher could only climb back into the saddle, aiming for Tejunga, sixteen miles distant, with the hollow, angry eyes on him.

"He ain't worth much if he can't find water, is he?" Sculls asked Denver, but the red-headed man didn't even glance at Sculls.

He rode wearily forward, his horse like a saw-edged rock beneath him. Denver found that he didn't really care about the gold at all just then. It was water, gushing streams of water, icy waterfalls of water which occupied his mind. He followed the straggling line of horsemen up the denuded canyon where a dead, weathered cedar hung over the trail.

It was sundown when they hit Tejunga—a red-walled box canyon where there had once been an Indian settlement. Now there was nothing but the crumbled adobes . . . and water.

They fell from their horses, staggering to flop face down into the trickle of brackish water which ran off the red stone bench higher up.

Crutcher sat aside, watching the sunset play on the fluted canyon walls, deepening the red in them, flooding the deeper ravines with shadow as the deep crimson flush spread across the utterly clear sky. It was still well over a hundred, absolutely dry.

"You're not thirsty, Mister Crutcher?" Ferguson asked.

"I am."

Ferguson was aware of a sharpness in the man's eyes, an edge to his words, and he nodded, leading his bay gelding away.

He waited until the others had had their fill, then he drank deeply, stripping his shirt to wash the dust from his muscle-knotted chest which was pale compared to the deep brown of his angular face. He rubbed the roan, speaking softly to it as it drank, utterly content with the coolness it nuzzled.

"Wren is boiling up the last of our coffee. Better come and have a cup before it's gone, the way the men are having at it."

Crutcher turned to Aston without answering. His hands moved in constant circles on the roan's back as he rubbed it with grass.

"All right. What is it, Crutcher?" Aston asked, crouching down beside him.

"Just an idea. You know, Yaqui Bob thought Thumb was riding for Conejo. Yet he couldn't have known. All he knew was that Thumb was riding west by south."

"Agreed," Aston replied thoughtfully.

"What I was thinking," Crutcher said, suddenly leaving off rubbing, "is that not far from here, up along the Abajos, there's a place with good water and a lot of grass where Thumb used to make winter camp years ago."

"So?"

"Nothing," Crutcher shrugged, "unless he's planning on making winter camp there again."

"This place," Aston asked, rising, "you know where it is?"

Crutcher's face was only an indistinct form in the growing darkness. He answered, "Yes I do. I helped Thumb find that camp."

"Helped him find it!" Aston laughed, incredulously.

"Yes, sir. Thumb hadn't ranged this far west before. I guess I know that country better than any man, red or white. I first showed him that little valley up there—it's hidden away in dry rock country. If a man didn't know it was there, he'd never guess. But there's a spring there, a good one. Pine trees—at that low altitude . . ."

"You can't believe he'd return there, knowing you're with us."

"That's just it, sir. He don't know I'm with you. He couldn't. All he knows is that a small force of soldiers is chasing him south and west. Now if he turned," Crutcher went on, sketching his meaning in the sand, "and swung north across that hard rock . . . well, there's not many could follow, and fewer yet who know of that valley."

Aston studied the drawing in the sand by match light and frowned. The match illuminated his serious features briefly, then burned out.

"But, if you are wrong, we'll be days more off the track," Aston commented.

"And if I'm right," Crutcher said, watching Aston in the darkness, "we're *ahead* of Thumb."

"I'll think on it, Crutcher."

Aston rose and strode through the darkness toward the camp. He wished that Ivory Hunter hadn't been wounded; Aston had trusted Ivory, valued his opinion.

There was a thin crescent moon rising over the horizon and Aston stood on a rocky outcropping watching it and the desert, glossed with its silver light.

It boiled down to the same old question—how much could he trust Crutcher?

To catch up with Thumb now, they would have to circle wide, then angle back sharply, hoping against hope that they could pick up three-day-old sign—doubtful in the desert which shifts daily, changing with the winds, the whims of nature. Yet he had to ask himself—who had brought them circling wide into the hills? Crutcher.

Could it be that Crutcher was still close to Thumb, his brother-in-law, and was laughing up his sleeve as he led the troop on a wild goose chase?

Aston picked up a handful of pebbles and

tossed them idly down the long slope. Perhaps Crutcher's share of the gold was larger than any reward, as repayment for leading this wild desert chase.

Now the man wanted to take them farther north, farther away from Thumb.

He asked Wren what he thought of Crutcher's idea and the big sergeant had to say frankly, "I don't know, sir. I guess only Crutcher really knows. But I doubt like hell we'll ever catch up with Thumb if we have to reverse our course now and go back out on the flats."

"Then there's the water to consider," Aston said.

"Yes. That too. Thumb's probably poisoned it."

"It doesn't leave us with much choice, does it, Wren?"

"Not much," Wren agreed, lifting his eyes to the young officer. "It's Crutcher's game—trust him or not, he's the only one knows a damned thing about this territory. If he's lying, we'll sure as hell lose Thumb. If he's tellin' the truth—we've a chance. A slender chance, mighty slender. But a chance."

"And you think he's telling the truth?"

"I do," Wren said. "He's a two-fisted, horn-backed ornery, horn-blowin' salty buck, but a liar . . . I never had Crutcher figured for that."

"I only hope you're right, Sergeant," Aston said slowly. "Because it doesn't appear we have any choice but to believe Crutcher, does it?"

They were out at daybreak, climbing higher

into the empty hills. The air grew no cooler as they rode upward, but only stronger, catching them with treacherous gusts as they scaled the shale-strewn upper valley and crossed the narrow, broken natural bridge between the two largest peaks, San Ignacio and El Capitan.

It was a full day, one without water, before they came into a gentle, hidden valley carpeted with grass, shaded here and there with stands of pine and cedar. A shallow creek trickled across the valley floor, winding through the grass.

They spotted a mule deer buck, too far off for a shot even had they wanted to risk one, and a large covey of quail, spooked up by the horses' hoofs.

The temperature here was moderate, the wind cut by the high-rising surrounding bluffs and the timber. Aston slowed the troop and circled back to where Crutcher rode.

"Thumb's camp?"

"Beyond those trees," Crutcher said.

"Ride lightly men, arms at the ready."

Yet, after they had wound through the pines and crested a grassy knoll, they saw nothing in the wedge-shaped valley below where Crutcher maintained there was a sweet spring.

Aston searched the valley with his field glasses, inch by inch, finding no trace of man or horse. When he turned to Crutcher, the man was grinning broadly.

"I don't see anything," Aston said impatiently. "And I don't find anything so amusing about it."

"You don't?" Crutcher said, wiping his sweaty hands on his jeans. "Hell, Aston, all this means is that we've done it. We've beaten Thumb up here. All we've got to do is sit down and wait, Lieutenant. You want to see some Apaches, you just wait, because you'll soon be seeing more than you ever wanted to."

Ten

Wren's nerves were nearly shot, and he wasn't alone. It had been three days since they came upon the hidden valley and concealed themselves and their horses high on the wind-swept rim.

They slept with one eye open, half-expecting to find an Apache hovering over them when they awoke. The men hardly spoke, but moved around silently, spending long hours staring at the forested valley below, alert to any movement, unusual patch of color, listening for the sound of a hoof on stone, a low voice . . . anything. Yet there was nothing.

Aston was grim, his rifle always near at hand, his field glasses constantly sweeping the meadows, the pine stands beyond.

"Nothing."

Wren was tight-lipped, lifting weary eyes to

Aston. "Nothing, damn it!" Aston stood up. "Where's Crutcher?" he demanded.

Wren nodded toward the whitish clump of boulders higher up on the ridge. Aston snatched up his rifle and began climbing toward the scout. It was a rough go, through manzanita, over sharp outcroppings, the wind batting at his back. Finally, huffing, he clambered up to where Crutcher sat cross-legged, eyes on the distances.

"Okay, Crutcher. All right . . ." Aston panted. "This is the third day!"

Crutcher stretched out a big hand and hooked Aston's knee, yanking him to a sitting position. Aston's face twisted with fury, but Crutcher put a finger to his lip, then pointed out onto the desert.

Aston squinted into the noon sun, seeing nothing. But he raised his field glasses, shielding the lenses from glare, and then he did. A string of horsemen winding through the low, broken foothills toward the valley. And they were Apache.

"Thumb!" Aston breathed, and with the word the realization came to him with finality that he would meet the Chiricahua; that this was no vague phantom moving toward them through the haze, but reality—a cunning, angry enemy.

"Do you see the kid?" Crutcher asked.

"Uh-uh." Aston adjusted the glasses, shook his head and handed them to Crutcher.

The boy was not visible, perhaps he was

97

farther back, but Crutcher recognized three men by their paint; the man, Thumb, and a tough undersized lieutenant named Bear Foot. Thumb's brother, a quiet, almost studious brave called Po-ah-Key, or Sand, was also visible.

"Come on." Crutcher slid off the rock, wanting now to be below the skyline where they could not be detected themselves. Together the two men sat on the sun side of a massive white boulder. A stream of red ants rushed across the earth at their feet.

"Now what?" Aston asked in a low voice.

"Sir—I reckon that's your decision," Crutcher answered, irony tinting his meaning.

Aston watched Crutcher without expression, then the officer pulled a broken cigar from his pocket and lit it, puffing shakily at it.

"What would *you* do?" Aston asked with a smile.

"Me? I guess I'd plan on talking, Lieutenant. Trying to bluff Thumb, maybe. He don't know how many men we have, unless he somehow knows we're the same party as those who were tracking him out of Cheer—and I don't think that's likely.

"Thumb's rugged and he's smart, but he's bringing a weary, small band of his men to this place of security. He won't want to fight, not unless it's necessary, if he thinks it'll be a fight to the death, that we've outnumbered him. Well," Crutcher shrugged, "maybe he'll talk trade, maybe not."

"If he doesn't . . . ?"

"Sir, you know what happens if he doesn't."

"Yes," Aston nodded, stubbing out his cigar, "I guess I do."

"I think talking's our only chance. Failing that," Crutcher said honestly, "we're dead men."

"Would he trade the boy for safe passage out of here—assuming he believes I've got a superior force?" Aston was turning the few alternatives over in his mind. "If I told him he could have the gold for the boy . . . would he likely take that offer?"

"I can't say," Crutcher replied. "You'd have to ask the man."

"And you, Crutcher—if it comes to that—would you let Thumb have the gold?"

"In a second, Lieutenant," Crutcher said. Then he rose and swung his rifle onto his back, climbing down the rocks to the camp where Wren was waiting, rifle in his thick fists.

"Remember all that extra ammunition you handed out to your boys?" Crutcher asked. "Best tell them it's time to break it out."

Po-ah-Key came silently through the forest, hearing the jays in the tall pines, the woodpeckers, the rustling of bough against bough without concentrating on the sounds. Beyond the quiet valley, the spring gurgled up pleasantly, a gift from the earth for the tired horses and their riders.

He shifted slightly on his pony's back, but

99

Thumb was still some hundred yards behind, leading his ragged legion.

Po-ah-Key sat on the very edge of the forest, his pony still in shadow. It was a quarter of a mile across the high grass to the spring which gurgled from the base of the white stone bluffs. A golden marmot shuttled through the grass, stopped to go to its haunches, studying the interloper, and scurried on.

It was silent, the breeze slight. He rode onto the grass, the breeze stirring the single feather in his hair, lifting his pony's mane.

Nothing moved. He rode slowly forward, his pony's hoofs bending the long grass. A lone high eagle floated through a cloudless sky.

Po-ah-Key slid from his pony's back and led the animal to the spring. The water gushed up from deep within the mountain. It was cold, frothed with aeration, sweet. Leaning his brass-studded rifle against a rock, he lay flat on his chest, drinking the water with cupped hand.

Having filled his belly, he rolled over on his back, breathing slowly, deeply . . . then he saw the shadow and he sprang to his feet, diving for his rifle, but the rifle was gone!

"Howdy, Sand."

Po-ah-Key blinked and blinked again. He had to look into the sun, but he thought that the man squatting carelessly on the rock above him was . . . no, impossible!

Yet it was. That grin, those harsh blue eyes. Po-ah-Key shaded his eyes with his hand.

"Howdy, Crutcher."

"Thumb just behind you?" Crutcher asked.

"A way, Crutcher," Po-ah-Key replied. He was tall for an Apache, thick through the chest, nearly as thick as Thumb himself. Thumb's brother was a quiet man, but a deadly hunter as Crutcher knew.

"I thought no man could steal up on me, Crutcher," Po-ah-Key said with grudging admiration, "let alone take my weapon."

"You weren't expecting it, that's all, Sand. We can all be taken, no?"

"Yes, Crutcher, we can all be taken." Po-ah-Key sat cross-legged on the grass, the spring bubbling up behind him, flowing out to lose itself in the grassy meadow. "And you—will Thumb take you? He hates you still."

"I know."

"He loved Morning Rain—as did I. He loved his nephew, Daniel. But you took them away to become white. Then the disease . . ."

"Cholera."

"The white disease took their lives. Thumb cannot forget it." Sand watched the tall man on the rock above him. He had always liked Crutcher; at one time they had been inseparable friends, hunting elk in the high country together . . . with Thumb. "My brother can have no sons, Crutcher."

"I know."

"And so he loved Daniel . . . but he will be here soon, Crutcher. Why have you come here? What is it you want from us now—after all this time?"

"I want to talk to Thumb. Under a flag of truce."

"He will not hear of it," Sand objected.

"Make him!" Crutcher shouted.

"I make Thumb do nothing. He is a wild thing, Crutcher. You know that." Sand tried to smile, but found he could not. He got to his feet and nodded toward the forest beyond. "He comes."

"Tell him I will come down tonight. With an army officer. To speak under a truce flag."

"The boy!" Sudden understanding illuminated Sand's lean face. "It is the boy you want."

"Yes. The boy." Crutcher stood on the rock. "He has a mother, Sand. A mother who has lost her husband and wants her only son back."

"He is Thumb's son—or will be."

"No. Thumb may say it, but it is not true. Tell Thumb what I have said. Tell him we will come down tonight—unarmed."

"He will kill you, Crutcher. No matter what, he will kill you."

"Maybe." Crutcher tossed Sand's rifle to him, then the tall man turned to disappear into the deep concealing brush.

"You are a brave man, Crutcher. Reckless." Sand held his rifle, his thumb on the hammer. "What if *I* had chosen to kill you?"

"It might have been difficult," Crutcher replied, "with no bullets in it."

Sand worked the lever once, smiled and watched as Crutcher sifted through the shadows and deep brush, disappearing as silently as any

Apache. Then he stood a long moment, his heart heavy. A time for dying had come upon them once more. And this time, one he loved would die.

Ferguson's head snapped up. The man had come upon them so silently. He noticed that Crutcher was wearing moccasins now.

Crutcher nodded to the Kentuckian, but said nothing, walking directly to where Aston sat nervously fingering his rifle.

"Well?" Aston asked.

Crutcher sat down beside him, took a swig from Aston's canteen and took off his hat.

"We're going to meet with Thumb."

"You spoke to him?"

"No—but I saw Sand . . . Thumb's brother. I told him we'd be coming down under a flag of truce. The two of us."

"And he agreed?"

"Oh, yeah," Crutcher grinned, "he agreed."

"We'll have safe conduct?" Aston pressed.

"Not exactly," Crutcher said. "I met Sand and told him we'd be coming under a white flag."

"But what did he say, Crutcher?"

"He reckoned Thumb would kill us," Crutcher said, and he was no longer grinning. "We're going to have to run us a good bluff, Lieutenant."

"But how—have you any ideas at *all?*" Aston asked. The young officer was upset, angry perhaps, but he had guts. There was determination in his eyes.

"Maybe one. If it will help or not, I can't say. We'll give it a try. Aston, this is the only way— talkin' with the man. Unless you want to try attacking his twenty-five with our seven."

"With the boy in between. No," Aston shook his head. "We'll try it, but if you've got an idea, you'd better drag it out now."

"I'll get on it," Crutcher nodded, sweeping back his sandy hair, poking his hat on. "I'll need some men—Wren, Ferguson, Benton."

"All right." The lieutenant watched Crutcher talking to Ferguson who nodded and got up. There was something about Crutcher—Aston could still not totally trust the man; he wondered idly if this meeting with Thumb were a ploy of some kind. Did Crutcher want that gold? He said Thumb hated him. Yet Aston wondered. Crutcher claimed he had simply walked down into that valley and spoken to an Apache warrior. It shouldn't have been that easy for a hated man.

Aston crawled to the edge of the rim and now, below, he could see the Chiricahuas setting up their camp. He watched them for a long minute, fascinated by this enemy which appeared tiny at that distance.

He edged back once more and sat in the hot sun, watching Wren and Ferguson with loads of wood under their arms, walking up to the north peak.

He suddenly pushed the doubts from his mind. He had come this far with Crutcher—and

104

without him he could go no further. It was their only chance, bad as it was. There was nothing for it but to back Crutcher to the hilt.

But he took an oath then and there. If it was a trap, a cheap trick, he would track Crutcher to the ends of the earth and kill him where he stood.

Eleven

It was coming dusk, the streamers of reddish clouds like battle flags against the deeper sky. There was a packet of thunderheads over the far mountains. Crutcher wondered disinterestedly if that would spill over onto the desert, bringing rain.

He watched the clouds a moment more, then studied the darkening sky. Abruptly he spun and walked to where Aston, gloves folded neatly over his belt, stood waiting.

"We'd better get started. After dark they'll never see our flag."

"Does it matter?" Aston asked, but Crutcher ignored the remark.

"Start those bonfires burning," he told Wren instead.

"I don't think they'll do any good, either," Aston said. Again Crutcher could only shrug.

"Maybe not. But if we're going to tell Thumb we've fifty men up here, let's at least make it look like it."

"Is that what we're going to tell him?" Aston asked. The young officer felt his stomach knotting as the moment approached; he neither heard the answers to his questions nor cared. Aston decided at this moment he would prefer bloody pitched battle to this insane diplomacy.

"Let's head on out," Crutcher said, and with a deep breath he began the sliding descent down the rock face; if he knew Thumb as he thought he did, there were already eyes upon them.

The descent was nearly straight down for fifty feet, then Crutcher led Aston out onto a gradually downsloping bench which he had used on his first trip. The bonfires sparked red against the deepening skies. A flight of doves winged past against the subdued fire of the sundown sky.

Crutcher strode carelessly across the dark meadow grass, Aston marching stiffly beside him. The bravado was for the benefit of the Chiricahua—they had no respect for a man who showed fear even when it caused his throat to constrict, his heart to race, the blood to pulse in the temples as it did now in Crutcher's.

"Almost there. Almost . . ." Crutcher said in a low voice as they approached the dark line of the woods where nothing was visible and no sound rose up. He counted this as a good sign, thinking that Thumb would have killed them on sight if he did not mean to interview them.

Unless, Crutcher thought ironically, Thumb wants to watch me get my throat cut with his own eyes.

They stepped into the timber, the heavy boughs of the towering pines blotting out what had been left of daylight.

"Which way?" Aston whispered tensely. Crutcher had halted.

"I think these gentlemen will show us the way," Crutcher said, and then Aston saw the line of Apache warriors in full paint closing a circle around them.

They were rushed through the forest, stumbling, falling, sliding before an escort of silent guards. Crutcher lost his footing once more, scrambled to his feet and was rushed along by two men, each holding an arm and a rifle.

Panting, his head spinning, he finally saw ahead a faint, shimmering light which grew larger and clearer as they burst into the open to face the gathering of Indians across a wind-twisted campfire.

They were shoved roughly across the clearing, a gun stock pushing against Aston's neck, and they stumbled rather than walked the last fifty feet to where a lean-to of pine boughs had been hastily thrown up.

Crutcher staggered forward, ducked to clear the entrance of the lean-to and stopped, chest heaving, muscles twitching.

Thumb sat across the fire ring, bare chested, his coal black eyes dancing with the fire. Sand was beside him, expressionless as well, and Bear Foot.

"Howdy, Thumb," Crutcher said, and incredibly he was grinning. "Heard you been kicking up some dust."

"Crutcher," Thumb said in a manner which merely acknowledged his presence. He glanced then at Aston, his mouth turning down with distaste. Thumb spat into the fire. "Armyman," he grunted as if the word itself had a sour taste.

"You better learn to like the army-men, Thumb," Crutcher said, "you'll soon be meeting a lot of them."

"So?" Thumb's mouth twisted into what might be called a smile. "How many, Crutcher?"

Aston couldn't speak for a moment, fascinated by the scarred, grisly face of Thumb. Around his neck he wore a silver and turquoise necklace which dangled to his bulky chest. In his rough, weathered hands, he toyed with a long-bladed knife which caught the firelight as he turned it. In the corner of the lean-to was a strong box with the Southern Pacific logo stenciled on it.

"Thumb," Aston said in a strained voice, "I have come to offer to you and your people a chance for freedom. My troopers are superior to yours in number, and they are fresh. We have been waiting here many days for you. . . ."

"How long will you speak?" Thumb asked with aggravation apparent in his husky voice.

Suddenly he leaped to his feet, catlike in his movements despite the bulkiness of his leg muscles and thick torso. He placed the cutting edge of the knife under Aston's Adam's apple and pressed slightly.

"In exchange for certain . . ."

"You want my gold. For my gold you will allow me to leave." Thumb's voice was bitter and Crutcher recognized the tone. The man had grown cynical during the years of battle, the long months of running, of going thirsty.

"Basically, yes," Aston managed to squeak. Thumb withdrew his knife with a gesture of contempt.

"But you would not attack me after I gave you the gold?" Thumb shook his head and spat. For a moment he was silent, staring at the fire. "And where would I run, Army-man? We have run as far as we can."

Crutcher had held his silence, knowing the animosity Thumb held toward him, but now he spoke up: "You can trust this man, Thumb. I know him and he will keep his word. His men will not attack if you return what you have taken."

Thumb exploded with brief laughter.

"You!" He waved the knife at Crutcher. "You would speak for another man's honesty? You who broke your promise to raise your son as an Apache?"

"Times where changing too fast, Thumb— you knew that. What did you want me to do? Let

Daniel ride the warpath with you?"

"No!" Thumb said suddenly, but it was not an answer to Crutcher, but to Aston's proposition. "I need the gold to buy guns, to clothe my people."

"All right." Aston nodded his head in agreement. "You may keep the gold. Keep the gold and ride out."

"I do not need your permission," Thumb said arrogantly.

"Yes. You will, I assure you. My soldiers surround your camp. We have cannon, Thumb," Aston bluffed.

Sand glanced at Crutcher, then at Thumb with anxiety in his eyes. He spoke rapidly in Chiricahua. "We cannot fight cannon, Thumb. If they are on that bluff above us . . ."

"Shut up!" Thumb said violently. "You forget the traitor speaks our tongue."

"I'm no traitor, Thumb. Just a man you once called brother."

"A brother who killed my sister and her son! A brother who brings the army-men to my camp." Thumb was silent for a moment. Bear Foot had said nothing, but he indicated with his eyes that he considered the proposition fair and necessary.

"We will take the gold," Thumb said. "And we will leave."

"There is another condition," Aston said.

"A condition?" Thumb rubbed his chin and his lips tightened.

"The gold and safe passage is yours—for the boy."

Thumb glared at Aston, his eyes fierce, his neck muscles twitching, but when he spoke, he spoke calmly.

"I have no boy."

"You have the boy," Aston insisted. "And we want him back."

"Or you will fight."

"Yes. We will fight and have both the gold and the boy. And your people, Thumb, will have only the cold earth to bury them." Aston was riding high on his bluff now; but Thumb had played poker with the white man before, and he knew that an ace in the hole can be speculated upon, but not considered when the time came to call. A fire on a hill did not mean that an army was waiting, poised there.

"I have no boy," Thumb said again. Perhaps he had caught a glimmer of uncertainty in Aston's eye, but he was no longer buying the bluff. Crutcher stepped forward and put a hand on Thumb's shoulder.

"I'll trade myself, Thumb. *I'll* stay if you let the boy go back to his mother."

Thumb's face wrinkled with suppressed laughter, then tightened to an animal fury.

"Did you think that I would let you go anyway, Crutcher? No! I have no boy, army-man. I will fight! That is my decision."

Crutcher's eyes met those of Sand across the fire. Sand's shoulders moved in an almost imperceptible shrug. He had warned Crutcher;

112

he could do nothing else.

"But you don't understand . . ." Aston said emotionally, and it was at that moment that the guns opened up.

Twelve

The night was a sudden wild thunderstorm, the thunder's roar the exploding guns close upon them, the deadly lightning the trail of bullets slashing through the darkness. Outside a brave screamed, a horse whinnied in mortal anguish. They were into the clearing, firing from every angle, clouds of black powder smoke obscuring the campfire. *Beamon!*

Aston whirled and shouted an oath just as Thumb slashed out with his knife, narrowly missing Crutcher's face. Then the Indian leaped across the fire, bolting for the entrance as a horse crashed through the wall of the lean-to, a hail of bullets spattering the interior.

Sand screamed and toppled over onto his face. Bear Foot had never moved. He sat cross-legged, half his skull blown away.

Aston screamed and Crutcher turned to see

the officer on his face, writhing, blood spilling from his arm. Crutcher snatched Sand's rifle from his dead hand and dove to barely elude the horse which had trampled down the side of the lean-to.

Crutcher levered three shots through the Winchester, hammering the shots home, and the horse and slicker-clad rider went limp and died in that deadly moment, filling the remains of the lean-to with blood, struggling flesh and rolling smoke.

A second horseman appeared and Crutcher fired an off-hand shot, leaping aside. He grabbed Aston by the collar of his shirt and dragged him from the lean-to.

The men were swarming over the camp, firing left and right. The fire had gone dead and, in the darkness, Crutcher stumbled over a still form.

Aston had gone under from the pain, but Crutcher dragged him into the timber, hastily burying him in the concealing pine needles. Then he crawled back to the camp, his own shoulder leaking blood from a shot he could not recall.

Beamon's nasty hawk face appeared in torch-light and Crutcher, in a fury, fired twice, taking the man from his saddle. He tried to circle back into the timber, but he was cut off. He fell back, trying to lever another cartridge in as the horseman hovered over him.

"Crutcher."

Crutcher recognized the voice at the same

instant he realized that he had been trying to fire an empty rifle.

"Remember, Crutcher?" Sculls said. Crutcher looked up in time to see the leering, dark face of Sculls over the sight of the rifle he had trained on him. Then the rifle muzzle exploded and he felt his head explode, the world going dark. There was the vague sensation of damp pine needles against his bloody face, the ringing laughter of Sculls. Then there was nothing.

He was lying face up under a black waterfall. Icy water roaring across him. He hardly cared—a blacksmith was drumming against his brain with a sledgehammer.

It was cold, but he did not feel like trying to move or build a fire. He doubted he would be capable of movement, the way a thought could rack his head with pain, the simple effort of trying to open an eye.

Hell—it was no waterfall, it was raining. Crutcher found that vaguely amusing. He was on his back in mud and leaf litter. His face was smeared with dirt, blood or both, his eyes open to the rain which was falling through the trees. A massive black pine overhead swayed against the dark sky. From far off he thought he heard a horse nicker, but there was no second sound and Crutcher closed his eyes, letting the coldness soak into him.

It's not dark anymore, he thought after a time, and when he opened one peering eye, he saw that he was right. Brilliant rays of sunlight cut

116

pathways through the pines. He was soaked clear through, his head shot through with fiery pain.

I can move, he told himself, but he didn't attempt it. Every movement increased the pain. He was cold. Cold. He tested his fingers and his toes. Wriggling them, he found they all worked and, smiling faintly, he fell off again into a troubled, restless sleep.

When he again opened his eyes, Crutcher could see a brittle, bright star peering through a gap in the high white clouds. It was coming dark again and his stomach was nagging him. Gingerly, he raised a hand and touched his scalp, finding it caked with blood, the hide peeled back. That touch cost him a violent shooting pain through his skull.

His shoulder, he was aware, was also wounded, but it caused only a little pain and it was powerfully stiff. He lay still, watching the star as the clouds swallowed it up.

Damn! It came to him suddenly, his thoughts focusing on what had happened, what his situation was. Beamon had attacked the camp. Thumb was gone. Aston had been wounded . . . or killed. Sculls had tried to blow his head off.

Crutcher sat up suddenly, his head reverberating with bells, flashing with dots of colored light. He was mad. Mad clean through.

"Sculls, you'll pay . . ." he muttered, but he hardly had the breath to finish his oath.

"If I had any brains I'd lay back and die," he panted. "If."

Crutcher got to his knees, holding his scalp with his right hand. With great difficulty, he got to his feet and the world went to spinning. He clung to a damp pine tree, waiting until it passed. Then he limped forward, surprised at how far from the camp he was . . . or maybe it just seemed like a long way with each step echoing in his skull.

The dead still lay in the clearing. An Apache he did not know lay face up, watching the sky much as Crutcher had, dead. Then Thumb had run—otherwise he would never leave his dead unburied.

The lean-to was trampled flat and Sand was still there along with Bear Foot—the gold was gone. Sand had been a good man. A violent man, perhaps, but it was the way of his people, his time. He would not go unhonored by the Chiricahua.

"So long, brother," Crutcher said. He bent over, head throbbing and took a rifle from the hand of Beamon's man. His horse still lay on top of him, wild-eyed in death.

With distaste, Crutcher turned the man's face to him, but he did not know the white either— just another nameless man who had gone out after some of that easy money.

Aston. He had left Aston concealed under some pine needles. But where? He could not force the memory to surface. Aston hadn't been wounded critically, but he had been bleeding and the wound was untended. Probably the exposure had finished the job, yet, with luck,

Aston might be alive out there.

Crutcher walked across the clearing, trying to recapture the memory. The horses had been trampling down the fire, men shouting, guns blazing in the darkness. Crutcher held his head.

Damnit, man. Think!

Why hasn't Wren come down? Crutcher asked himself. Perhaps Wren had gone after Beamon or Thumb.

Aston. Fuzzily his thoughts came together and he searched along the camp perimeter, finding another dead white man.

He stood in the darkness finally, studying the bank which fell off below him. *There*, he was sure. But Aston was no longer there.

Crutcher hobbled forward and got to his knees, searching the pile of pine needles until he found it—blood on a handful of dry litter. So Aston was here, but had gotten away.

Or maybe Wren had found him and not found Crutcher who was farther from the camp, unconscious so that he would hear no calling.

The rain had begun again, slowly, gently. The trees were glassy with drops of water and now they began swaying in the breeze which was picking up once more.

Crutcher clambered up the slope and stood numbly in the center of the camp. Now what?

He had no idea and his foggy mind could not order the priorities. *There was a horse*, he told himself with excitement. There had been a faint nickering. Yet that horse might be miles distant now. Worse yet, perhaps it had a rider.

119

The rain was increasing, a hard driving wind behind it. He would find nothing that night, he knew, and he began looking for some sort of shelter, the rifle he had taken from the dead man protected under his stained buckskin jacket.

A brief, brilliant spate of lightning and thunder rolled past and walking, head down, Crutcher discovered what he would not normally have found.

In a relatively protected area, where a gigantic smooth boulder sat among a stand of young pine, there was the clear sign of a pony and of the man who had ridden him—an Indian by the moccasins. And as another flash of lightning crackled through the night, Crutcher saw beside these footprints the small imprints of moccasins made to fit a child's feet.

Thumb had the boy and a horse. He was long gone.

Crutcher dragged himself back into a cleft in the boulder where a young cedar sent out tentacles of root, searching for soil. There, in that web of root, in the cold of the rain, he slept, rifle in hand.

Morning was brilliant, the deep forest stretching wide beneath a clear sky. Crutcher was up and moving, painfully, slowly, but moving.

He made the springs in an hour, and he shed his filthy clothing and slipped into the icy water, washing the trail dust, the blood, the stink of death from him. Shivering on the bank, clad only in his buckskin pants, he dabbed at his

120

scalp with a cloth torn from the tail of his shirt.

He had a constant ringing in his skull, a dull, insistent headache, but the sledgehammer pounding was gone now and the cloth came away bloody, but not saturated with heavy bleeding.

He had stuffed himself with some currants and eaten a handful of bulbs from some sego lilies, quieting his hunger somewhat. Now he filled his belly with the icy, sweet water, wishing for a canteen. He knew well how far it was to the next source of water, though with the rain there might be pools left here and there, where there were rocky basins.

Dressing, he walked the meadows until he came to the high bluffs where the bench led to the rocky chute he had come down.

It cost him more blood and exhausted his meager resources, but Crutcher finally rolled up onto the bluffs where the camp had been.

Then he saw why Wren had never come down.

The death rain had fallen here, too. Corporal Benton was dead, still wrapped in his blanket. Wren had a knife in his back, and beneath him lay White—his head twisted crazily on a broken neck. Sculls' henchman had underestimated the strength of Wren and he had paid the price.

Crutcher shook his head bitterly at the grim little scene. For some reason, looking at Wren now, he thought of the terrific left hook the man had possessed and which he had used once to floor Crutcher.

"You could fight, Sarge," Crutcher said quietly.

He searched the camp, but saw nothing else until he looked down the bluffs. Ferguson. The Kentuckian had been killed too, his body thrown over the cliff.

Crutcher sagged onto a rock, exhausted, sick at heart. Sculls had pulled off this little massacre which coincided with Beamon's attack on Thumb's camp.

"I told you not to turn your back on Sculls," Crutcher said bitterly, his head hanging, still filled with pain.

Standing, he dragged himself back into the camp, picking up a canteen which he meant to fill at the springs. He knew he hadn't the strength to bury these men—men who had died for nothing, murdered by their own kind.

"I'm sorry boys, I just ain't got it in me." He stood there a moment longer, canteen dangling by its strap from his hand. Then he turned and slid back down the bluffs, his stomach knotted.

After filling the canteen at the springs, Crutcher started walking. There were still a few hours of daylight left. His brain thundered with pain, but he put it out of his thoughts, taking a step at a time.

Thumb was gone, undoubtedly thinking that Crutcher had planned out that ambush, hoping to get the boy and the gold—the Chiricahua would never again trust a white flag.

Aston was gone, presumably badly wounded, afoot—the desert would likely kill him even if he had been lucky enough to find a horse.

Crutcher was coming down the eastern slope of the peak called El Capitan. The chocolate-covered mountain was rugged, barren. Drift sand stretched tentacles up hundreds of feet in the canyons, streaking the landscape oddly. He paused out of breath on a ledge, studying the broad desert—a land he knew as well as any man alive; a land which had never before frightened him.

Just now it scared him silly.

Crutcher spent the night huddled on that narrow ledge, high up where the cold winds blew, and the night long, he studied on his situation.

He wanted the boy.

He wanted to find that little boy and take him back to his mother. Yet Thumb had him, and Thumb had the capacity to run, to fight, to hide in places where it would be difficult to extract him—like a chuckawalla which will crawl into a cleft in the rocks and then puff up its scaly body so that you couldn't yank it out with a mule team.

In his present condition, Crutcher had no chance of catching the man. Sick, afoot, without a soul to help him . . . the idea was crazy.

A man can run a horse down, a good man in good condition, but Crutcher was traveling hurt. Thumb was as desert-wise as he was, and abler just now.

Crutcher closed his eyes a moment, then

opened them to the star-flecked sky. It was flat impossible, and he knew it.

A sheer white cloud drifted past the white half-moon.

All right! What about Sculls?

The idea came to him with sudden impact. Up until that moment, he had given no real thought to Sculls, except for holding that vague impulse for revenge.

What about Sculls?

Beamon was dead—Crutcher had shot him during the raid—the only satisfaction he had from that bitter night. That left Sculls in charge of the Beamon gang, probably. There was Reg Quailer, but the big man had always been soft-brained, unwilling to accept any responsibility.

Excitedly, Crutcher pursued the thread of his thought.

Thumb he could not run down, could not fight. But the desert was his ally against Sculls. Beamon might have ridden any number of directions, cooling his heels. But Sculls was a different matter—a deserter, and a man of limited knowledge of the area. He would run south, toward the border.

That seemed intelligent, but Crutcher knew it was the most rugged terrain on God's earth. Any wounded they had with them would likely perish, some of the horses for want of water. And they were carrying the gold.

He had only to circle El Capitan's southern base, and he was sure he could cut their sign. After all—Sculls knew the soldiers were dead and believed that Crutcher was dead as well. He would be expecting no pursuit.

They would be on that broad, raw desert, weakening each day. While Crutcher grew stronger. He fell off to sleep then, a faint smile on his lips.

Thirteen

Ivory Hunter's head snapped up at the sound. He had been sitting by the window of the adobe, enjoying the pleasant warmth of morning sunshine. His chest was bound tightly and the wound itched some. Outside of that, he was as comfortable as he could recall ever being.

He had spent hours simply dozing at that window; his long silver hair spread over his shoulders, listening to the singing of Yolanda, watching her busy hands. The woman had changed rapidly, as if some baptism had found her on that desert. She rushed past him now to the door, wearing a black skirt, a plain white blouse, her raven hair knotted at the base of her neck and set off by a huge, pearl-inlaid comb, the only ornamentation she wore.

The muffled sound again reached Ivory's ears.

"Just a moment," Yolanda called. She grasped the latch and opened the massive wooden door.

He stood there, gasping for breath, his clothing ripped to shreds, his blood dripping down his pantleg. Then he opened his eyes wider and toppled to the floor as Yolanda gasped.

"Aston!" Ivory Hunter hurried to help the woman lift the officer onto a cot where she cut away his shirt, revealing a terrible wound in the upper arm.

"That's a bad one," Ivory winced.

The arm was broken, discolored to a greenish purple. Blood leaked from the wound which had scabbed, then been torn open numerous times. Aston's head rolled from side to side in fever, dark whiskers covering his sunburned cheeks.

"Lucky if he does not lose it," Yolanda said. She worked at the arm, cleaning it with cloths boiled in water. Ivory could only stand aside, leaning heavily on a cane as the woman worked, clucking as she did so.

Yet they shared a common thought—what had happened? To Aston, the troop . . . to Crutcher?

Yolanda worked feverishly, disinfecting the arm, yet there was a haunting pallor to Aston's face and the discoloration, the odor of the wound, prompted Ivory to say it.

"It'll have to come off."

"I cannot . . ." Yolanda stood and turned her back, patting her hair nervously. Then she spun back, face set.

"I'll do it," Ivory volunteered.

"Maybe . . ." Yolanda clutched Ivory's arm, yet they both knew it was the only way. Aston had gangrene. It would spread, killing him, unless the arm was amputated.

"I'll do it," Ivory said, holding Yolanda by the shoulders. "It won't be my first one."

Ivory's long Bowie knife was thrust into the flames of Yolanda's cooking fire while Ivory rolled up his sleeves and looked more closely at the young officer's arm, assuring himself of what he already knew.

It was over in minutes. Aston had gone under from the pain and he was breathing raggedly, his face absolutely pale.

"I think he'll make it," Ivory Hunter said.

Yolanda, shaken by what she had witnessed, walked out with Ivory to the well where he scrubbed up. The sky was darkening over Descanso and she shivered slightly, watching the far sky, the long empty land.

"Where can Crutcher be?" she asked softly, as if she were not speaking to Ivory at all.

"He's out there still. If anyone could make it, he will," Hunter said, reassuring her with words he did not believe.

It was two days before Aston came around fully. Ivory, who was nearly healed up himself, stood near the window and he heard Aston muttering as he had been when suddenly the man sat bolt upright and looked at his arm as if he had known all along that he would not find it.

"Damn." Aston lay back, biting at his white lip. "Damn it."

Aston's face twisted into anguished tightness for a moment, then released. He noticed Ivory Hunter standing over him and asked, "You do it, Ivory?"

"Yes, sir. It was gangrene."

"I figured as much. I lost all sensation and then . . ." Aston's voice broke off and he sat perfectly still a moment, eyes brooding.

"You found Thumb, sir?" Ivory asked, not liking the distant look in the lieutenant's glazed eyes, the tilt of his head.

"Yes. Found him." Aston was staring at the doorway and Ivory turned to see Yolanda, a water bucket in her hand, standing there. "We found Thumb," Aston said, still staring at Yolanda, his voice oddly sing-song.

"Crutcher . . . ?" Yolanda asked, advancing a step, her eyes wide. She was unable to contain the question any longer, but at her word Aston began trembling, raising a finger which he jabbed like a weapon.

"Crutcher," he spat, "ambushed us. He had men following us. He over ran the camp, after killing Wren and the others. Crutcher!" Aston said, his teeth clenched, working against themselves, "ran off with Thumb, taking the gold, and the boy."

"It can't be . . ." Yolanda said.

129

"It can't! It *is* true. Crutcher's men and the Apaches slaughtered us. Only I survived . . . I must have slipped away. I awoke wounded, it was cold . . . they were gone," Aston said, falling into an exhausted sleep. Yolanda and Ivory Hunter did not speak for a time, their eyes locked across the bare room.

Ivory nodded his head toward the door and Yolanda went outside, leaving Aston who was rolling in nightmarish sleep.

"It's impossible," Yolanda said.

"Yes. But there were other men out there. Crutcher told me it was Jasper Beamon and his crowd. Aston apparently thinks they were Crutcher's men. Crutcher slipped off to have a look at Beamon one night," Ivory explained, "and Aston might have thought it was a meeting."

"But he doesn't know Crutcher. Not like I do. We can explain it . . . if he'll listen."

"That's just it," Ivory said, studying the dark-eyed girl. "He won't. And *he* was out there. He'll report it like this back at Bowie and Crutcher will be shot on sight."

"No. A reasonable man . . ." Yolanda began.

"That's just it, Yolanda," Ivory guessed, "Aston's not quite reasonable just now. Did you see the way his eyes focus, or fail to? The way he spoke—I think the pain and shock have had an effect on his mind."

"We'll have to go back with him then," Yolanda insisted.

"Yes. We'll take him back to Bowie when he's

130

able." Ivory smiled faintly, holding a trembling Yolanda. "But it might not do much good for us to speak for Crutcher. We're friends of his, we know him—but only Aston was there."

Yolanda stepped back. "Do you think he's alive?"

"Sure," Ivory said. Yet if he was, where was Crutcher? And if he was alive now, perhaps he would be better off to keep running. Because if Aston was believed, Crutcher would be run up against a wall and shot dead.

Already the heat had returned to the desert, the rain waters seeping rapidly into the sand, leaving only a few damp patches. The lone man jogged silently southward, his head ringing with bells, his body sticky from the heat, his eyes red, gritty.

Crutcher had cut sign easily, and to follow the eight horses across the sand the rock earth was no problem at all. They trampled the earth like a herd of buffalo. Thumb would have laughed at such men.

The sun was dead overhead, refusing to go down, to cool the earth. Stumpy shadows lay flat under the outspread arms of giant saguaro cactus. And Crutcher ran on, dog trotting as the Apache would, his pace not killing, but steady. When younger, whole, he had once run twenty-seven miles in the heat of summer, drinking from his horse intestine water bag as he ran.

This . . . this was different. His head hurt, his arm throbbed. The hot sand scorched his feet, his breath tore at his lungs. But he ran, and after he had run an hour the pain ceased, the thought ceased. He simply ran, his long legs moving mechanically. He had one thought—to move faster than a walking horse.

Crutcher jogged on, the land rising and falling beneath his feet which were torn by sharp rocks. He opened the canteen as he ran, taking a swallow of the spring water. There was little enough of it left.

His rifle was hot in his hand, the metal of the receiver like an iron in his palm.

Come on! He encouraged himself constantly, bringing the face of Sculls to mind, forgetting all else but Wren's dead face, the smell of his own hair burning from powder.

Come on! His legs wobbled, grew rubbery. He wanted to travel at night this night, rising with the coming moon, running through the cool hours. It was a madman who ran beneath the sun, but Crutcher needed to close the distance. To do something a horse would not do, or be forced to do by its rider.

When he could go on no longer, he collapsed in the meager shade of a blue paloverde tree, taking the beans from the pods to eat. The Apaches used these beans as a staple for making a sort of bread, and Crutcher had dined on them before—bitter, slightly sulfuric, they were, nevertheless, nutritional, filling.

The sun was in his eyes, a demon sun cursing all men who entered this domain of the sun. Yet Crutcher had smiled at demon suns before, and he did so now, closing his eyes for a brief rest.

It was utterly dark when he awoke. He had not intended to sleep so long, but his body demanded it. Now he rose, stuffing the last of the paloverde beans into his pockets.

His legs were frozen stiff. The half moon dragged itself up from the bed of the eastern mountains, and Crutcher moved out slowly, picking the sign from the sand and rock.

As he warmed, his pace quickened and he ran easily through the bitter night, breath steaming from his lips as he cursed Sculls and his kind.

Twice during the night he fell, sprawling into deep, unseen depressions. Once he had torn his knee badly on a huge barrel cactus, the thorns breaking off deep inside his leg.

Yet he ran on. Sculls did not know the determination of this man or he would have stood over him, emptying his gun.

Determined—or was he mad?

Crutcher's head filled with wild thoughts during the long, torturous hours. Flames seemed to leap out of the sands, some of them with disfigured faces of those he knew, some with voluptuous figures, babbling lips which made no sound . . . at one point he simply collapsed and fell to an exhausted sleep.

When he awoke, the moon was high. With a start, he sat up. Something was chewing at his leg. A slavering beast and Crutcher lashed out with the stock of his rifle. The coyote slunk away into the night and Crutcher sat there in a cold sweat.

"You're crazy, my friend," Crutcher told himself again.

Yet, minutes later, he heard something far to the south or thought he did. He stood and listened closely, and after a time it came again—a horse. Crutcher stood watching the sunrise spreading an orange blanket across the dunes, a brief, brilliant flash of color before the sun rose once more, bringing the fierce heat.

He could run no more and, though he knew he was losing time, he slept. Waking after two hours, he dug into the sand at the base of an ironwood tree and found a seep of muddy water left from the rain. He sucked greedily at the silt-laden water, then slept another hour.

He found young yucca in flower. Their blossoms were nutty in flavor, yet tender and he ate several handsful.

Then he ran. He ran until it seemed that all of life had been a long run into the empty expanse of a yellow and red desert. The tracks before him were clearer now, more recent, and it inflamed his determination.

Crutcher's lips were swollen and split, his feet blistered and bleeding, his eyes red-rimmed and raw. A specter crossing an endless sea of sand. Yet, he had his reality to cling to—the memory of death and the solid weight of the Winchester in his right hand.

That day, he ran through the sunlight hours and into the darkness once again, stopping for brief, panting rests. He felt detached from his body. It was simply an instrument which when

134

he said "run," ran.

The country was deep dunes now, running nearly impossible. The sand, swirled and piled by the winds, shimmered blue beneath the moon. Some were a hundred feet high and Crutcher struggled through them, trying to find the easy way—yet there was none. Once, in Colorado, he had traveled through a bleak, awful landscape where the dunes rose up to nearly seven times the height of these rippled dunes. There were stories in that part of the country of men and horses, wagon trains which had sunk into those behemoth dunes never to be seen again.

He paused suddenly, thinking he was seeing things again. Like those flames which had flared up out of nothing the day before.

Yet this was no illusion. A dull reddish glow lit the deep purple sky near the horizon and Crutcher could smell, quite distinctly, wood smoke.

He stood still, limp, shocked by it. Shocked by success. It was an impossible task to catch up with Sculls afoot, yet it seemed he had . . . who else could it be?

He moved in a slow arc downwind—he wanted no horse to give him away—and crept forward up the still-warm dunes, spotting the campfire at the crest of the sand mountain.

He knew he was moving soundlessly on the sand and was invisible to the men whose eyes were fire-dulled. The horses could not scent him and so he took the chance of creeping closer yet.

Eventually, he was so near that he could see the unshaven faces of the men and, one after the other, he etched them in his memory for not one would get away with this.

Denver was there—the red-haired man wore his arm in a sling. Reg Quailer's massive form sat hunched near the fire, and beside him, Sculls.

Impulsively, Crutcher drew his rifle to his shoulder. He could get three of them before a man could move; yet he did not want it that way.

He waited, searching the dunes; but there was no guard posted. There were only six men left of the Beamon-Sculls gang. They must have lost more than they counted on in the Apache raid.

Two of them slept now, and soon the others must sleep. Their eyes were raw as well, for there is no easy passage on the desert.

Crutcher studied the camp closely. The men's gear was stacked to one side, the low fire built flat on the sand. Sculls was sitting on the gold crate, the horses off to one side, restlessly pawing at the sand, finding no forage. Crutcher smiled.

He rolled back to the far side of the dune, watching the stars, knowing what he must do. It was no trick at all for an Indian, especially not an Apache. The men below him were hard cases, well-armed fighting men, but they were not Indians, not wilderness-wise in the sense that the early mountain men had been. They trusted to their guns . . . but guns are only as useful as the man behind the trigger.

Crutcher glanced at the stars once again, judging the time. He would wait another two hours—until just before dawn.

Sculls had been sleeping fitfully. His shoulder and ribs were banged up from the scuffle with Ferguson. Their water lately had been that dredged out of ponds left from the rain, their food, jerky and sourdough. Their beds, the dunes or hard rock.

Yet they couldn't be five miles from Mexico, and Sculls allowed himself a narrow smirk as he thought of the women, the liquor, the soft beds he could now afford.

Unable to sleep any longer Sculls rolled out, his eyes sweeping the men. There were six of them, and he mentally divided the gold among them. He did not like the figure he came up with, yet there was little he could do about it just now.

Denver sat down beside Sculls on the crate, poking the dead fire to life.

"How far?" the redhead asked.

"Five miles. No more than ten."

"What about . . . ?" Denver nodded toward the big man, Reg Quailer.

"We'll worry about it later," Sculls said in a low voice. Denver shared a common mind with Sculls at times, it seemed. He had been doing his own computations. The red-haired man glanced at Sculls, measuring the man, those calculating eyes. He was glad Sculls was on his side.

Quailer was up, tugging on his boots. He

wore no shirt, and the muscles on his massive shoulders bulged. The sky was gray with the faint light of false dawn and Quailer made the rounds, poking the rest of the gang awake.

"Stay alert, Thomas," he grunted. "We'll be in Mexico today with luck."

Then Quailer's eyes flickered to Sculls who looked down at his feet. Sculls ran the words of Quailer quickly through his mind. *Stay alert*— maybe the big man wasn't as stupid as Sculls had thought.

Thomas, the pale Virginian, came rushing to the fire and he wore a look of blatant fear on his chalky face.

"Reg!" he called to Quailer. "The horses— they're gone!" The man was badly shaken. "The water with them."

For a moment, Quailer stood there, stunned. He started to smile, couldn't, and rushed toward the picket line where the ponies had been. Sculls was on his heels, rifle in hand.

"Damn!" Denver breathed.

They could only stand there dumbly a moment as the first rosy hues of dawn stained the dunes. Gone. They were gone! Hoofprints led up the yellow dunes beyond the picket line, then faded in the soft sand.

"Come on!" Sculls yelled and he took off at a run, sinking to his knees in the soft sand, five frantic men behind him.

"Damn!"

They crested the dune and stood panting, searching the far distances. Nothing—not a spot of color which was not of the desert.

"They could be just behind that dune," Denver said.

"They could be," Quailer said softly, "or just behind the next one. Or the one beyond that. Or that one . . . or that one." The big man shook his head. "They're gone."

"Who do you figure?" Thomas asked.

"Indians. Who else? They wanted them horses. It sure as hell wasn't the army," Quailer replied. He turned and trudged down the dunes, the rising sun laying a line of gold along the horizon, the broken mountains far to the east.

"What'll we do now?" the Virginian asked, his pale face frankly frightened.

"Keep on," Reg Quailer growled. "It ain't that far. We'll keep on, right Sculls?"

"We'll keep on—with our eyes open," Sculls said with that crooked smile.

Quailer himself hefted the gold chest. He believed it had been Indians—yet what if it was Sculls who had taken the horses? He cursed the day Beamon had met up with Sculls and taken the dark man in on this.

Then they began, without putting the fire out, leaving saddles and half their gear—thinking only of that imaginary line of the border which stretched across the desert somewhere beyond the dunes.

Ahead of them—to the south where the dunes flattened and then gave way to red, brush-sprinkled earth which rose to higher mesas, the buckskin-clad man sat an unsaddled gray horse, watching them.

"It's comin' time, Sculls," Crutcher said to the tiny struggling figures walking toward him. "It's comin' judgment time."

Fourteen

It was close to a hundred and twenty, hotter on the surface of the dunes. Sculls struggled up the long dunes, his body leaking sweat. He cursed with each step.

They plunged in to their knees, fought free and slid back three steps for every two they took forward.

"Five miles," Sam Denver panted. "Yet how far have we come since morning—half a mile?"

"Shut up."

Quailer had tried shouldering the gold chest on his own massive back, but had given up after a few hundred feet. Now Thomas, the Virginian, and another man called Freize took their turns trying to drag that awkward, heavy chest up the sandy slopes.

"We ought to split it up," Freize panted. "It would make the going easier."

"No!" Sculls said harshly, and for once Quailer agreed with him.

"Keep it together," Reg Quailer puffed. He was sitting on the sand, his massive forearms over his knees.

"Where's O'Rourke?" Thomas asked, suddenly aware that a man was missing. Denver met his glance and together they looked behind them. The Irishman was gone.

"Go have a look," Quailer panted.

"You go have a look," Thomas shouted back. The pale Virginian was frightened of the bear, Quailer, and never had spoken a harsh word to the man. Just now he was tired, hot and a little frightened. If there were Indians around, he had no intention of recrossing those dunes to look for O'Rourke.

"Forget it," Quailer mumbled, "he'll catch up."

"Let's keep moving," Sculls said. "Anybody got any water—I'm strangling on my tongue."

If anyone had it, he wasn't sharing and Sculls could only curse silently and walk on, he and Denver taking their turn with the heavy trunk.

"That wasn't such a bad idea—splitting up the gold," Denver said.

"Not if you're satisfied with the split," Sculls grumbled. "Keep it together."

"What about Quailer?"

"He's got his ideas, too," Sculls hissed. He had no breath left to speak any more. They crested the burning dune and half slid, half plunged down the opposite slope, Sculls

142

wrenching his knee as he slammed to a tumbling halt.

Sculls was cursing violently, holding his leg, as Quailer came down, spraying hot sand.

"Now what's the matter?"

"What the hell do you think—I hurt my knee!"

"Tough," Quailer said. "Keep moving, Thomas."

"We can spare a rest!" Sculls screamed.

"No—if we don't find some water, we're done. We can't sit out here. If you can't keep up—sit there and die."

Sculls sat sullenly as Quailer stormed on, slipping up the hill. Denver was with him, Thomas and Freize dragging the trunk.

Coolly Sculls pulled out his pistol, sighted it on Quailer's back and pulled the trigger, the roar of the gun rolling across the dunes.

Quailer turned, clutched at his chest, tried to bring his rifle up and then buckled at the knees, sliding face first down the dunes until he stopped, arms thrown out, his blood staining the sand.

Freize and Thomas had been unable to react, burdened with the chest and Sculls now walked toward them, dark hair in his glazed eyes.

"I think we can rest a while, don't you?" Sculls asked.

"I reckon," Freize nodded.

Sculls' gun was still on them. He motioned to Denver who scurried up the slope.

"Take their guns. Boys—" he explained as

Denver took their weapons and threw them away, "this is my gang now. It's up to you if you want to be a part of it."

"I reckon we'll stick," Thomas said, spitting.

"Good. We'll sit a time, then move on. You boys are doing fine with that trunk," Sculls said, sharing that rattler's smile with Denver. "Why don't you just keep on carrying it. All the way to Mexico."

"The hell!" the Virginian exploded. "We'll never make it."

"You quittin' the gang?" Sculls asked. He rocked back the hammer of the Colt he carried and the Virginian shook his head.

"I guess I'll stick," he said nervously. He knew he was playing with a rattlesnake now, and he meant to say nothing that would cause Sculls to strike.

"Take that canteen," Sculls said, and Sam Denver slipped Thomas's canteen strap off his shoulder, flipping it to Sculls who shook it, then smiled and took a deep drink, tossing the canteen back to Denver who did the same.

"You can't treat us like pack animals!" Freize shouted. "We'll die without water, carrying this gold."

"I reckon," Sculls said, his voice metallic. "But you got your choice. Die that way, or here and now. I didn't here anybody speak up for me when Quailer wanted to leave me."

Thomas nodded, glancing at Reg Quailer. The big man had seemed invincible, and in a fraction of a second he had died. He lay

144

sprawled, motionless on the white sand.

"Well!" Sculls demanded.

"We'll stick," Thomas said, feigning a smile.

"Good. Give my knee a minute, then we'll move on. Don't worry, men—we'll be in Mexico tonight, and we'll all have a bigger share."

"Sure," Thomas said, but already he knew he would never see Mexico.

They trudged on through the inferno of the day, the moments draining the strength from them. Thomas and Freize, laboring under the weight of the gold, moved like zombies across the sand. Thomas, whose complexion was normally pale, was now crimson in the face, his knees buckling at each step as thirst and hunger overwhelmed his vigor.

Time and again the bandits fell. The sun burned their faces, the weight of the gold pressed them into the sand. Once Freize misstepped, fell, and the trunk landed on his back, nearly crushing his spine.

Sculls merely waited, his gun in hand, letting the men struggle to their feet, flinty indifference in his eyes. Yet thirst was wearing on him as well.

Denver felt as if his mouth was filled with sand, burning his tongue and throat, trickling into a withered stomach.

"We got to find some water," Denver muttered to Sculls.

Sculls did not answer. What answer could he give?

There might be water somewhere on that

yellow sea of sand, but they had no idea where to look, how to find it. They stumbled on, senses dulled by the trek, flesh tortured by the sun.

There was a flat, reddish mesa filmed with the green of grass far off to the south. There would surely be water there, Sculls thought—but he had no way of knowing.

He hobbled on, cursing his painfully swollen knee with each step.

It was only five miles—less now. Three, say. Three miles to freedom. And he would be wealthy for the rest of his life . . . Sculls managed an oily smile.

From the caprock of the jutting mesa, the tall, sandy-haired man watched the ragged band struggle on through the dunes.

He sat on the very rim of the red mesa, sipping cool water from a water bag. The seven horses he had with him contentedly cropped grass behind him.

Crutcher got to his feet, stretched and walked to the horses, feeling better than he had in a week. He picked out the buckskin and slipped onto its back, gathering up the lead line to the string.

"Let's get some exercise," Crutcher said to the horses.

Fifteen

It was dark, silent. The earth underfoot was still warm from the day's heat although the moon was already rising above the dark silhouette of the mountain range to the east.

They had broken from the dunes just after sunset, and had trudged over the rocky, brush-spattered landscape for another mile until Sculls decided they were into Mexico without any doubt. Then they collapsed wearily into a desultory camp.

Freize was dead. He had gone down to stay three hours before. The Virginian, Thomas, sat in the darkness, watching Sculls, knowing it was only a matter of time until his hour came.

Sam Denver, beaten down by the day's work, lay on his back trying to sleep, but sleep would not come. After Freize had gone down, it had fallen to Denver to help with the gold.

Denver had been with Sculls for two years, yet he had never trusted the man—not after seeing the things he had done. Denver pondered his own situation a while. He had his gun, his strength—unlike Thomas who had been robbed of both and might not survive the night.

Sculls treated him like a pack animal as well. What would happen the first time Sam turned his back, slept too deeply? He thought he knew, and so he lay there, afraid to sleep.

It was an hour or so later when he heard a providential sound. Sculls was snoring loudly, gun in hand, deep in an exhausted sleep. Just beyond the pile of rocks and sumac above the camp, Sam Denver had heard, or thought he had heard, a horse nicker gently.

He started to sit upright, his body rigid, yet the red-haired man controlled that impulse, rolling his head slightly to look at Sculls who still snored, his eyes riveted shut by weariness.

Slowly Denver sat up. Thomas, tied to a broken mesquite bush, half dead from exhaustion, lay silently on the sand. The horse nickered again and Denver slid from his blanket.

Gun in hand, he slipped through the darkness. Once he knocked his knee against an unseen rock and his body filled with cold pain, but Denver muffled his exclamation to a grunt, limping on.

A horse could mean freedom. It could also mean danger. He moved warily through the brush, eyes flickering ahead and behind. He didn't want to run into any Apaches.

Then it was there.

Denver stood frozen, unbelieving. A gray horse he recognized as Reg Quailer's. Denver crouched low, watching silently for a long moment. The horse watched him, ears pricked. There was no other movement, no other sound in the darkness.

Gradually, gathering his courage, Denver stepped forward, taking the horse's bridle.

Silently he led it back toward the camp, keeping an eye over his shoulder. He paused at the camp perimeter, heart pounding wildly. Sculls still slept, or seemed to, the gold within ten feet of him.

"If he wakes up, I'll say I've come to tell him about the horse," Denver told himself. Yet he wondered if his eyes would reveal the lie, even in the darkness. Once he laid a hand on that gold, there was no backing out. Sculls would kill him coldly, with no more compunction than he would have about stepping on a spider.

Denver eased into the clearing, listening with heart hammering in his throat to the steady snoring of Sculls. Suddenly, taking determination from his desperateness, Denver crossed the clearing, nearly at the foot of the sleeping Sculls, and grasped the gold chest, dragging it into the brush, one hand cradling his revolver as he moved.

It was silent in the brush, silent in the camp. Perspiration chilled Denver's flesh and he dragged the crate more quickly toward the horse . . . It had been right there! It was gone.

Desperately, he looked around. In the darkness, perhaps he had grown confused. He knew he had tied the gray securely.

He dragged the trunk uphill, then circled, growing more anxious with each foot he moved. Sculls would kill him if he could—Denver had stepped over the line. He had to run. There was no explaining this.

The horse! Damn—he was sure . . . Denver stood, breathing heavily. It was gone. Just gone.

The gold was there, just under his hand. The means of escape had been there . . . Denver hastily covered the heavy trunk with brush and, panting, moved over and among the rocks, searching for the horse. Dawn was graying the eastern sky and panic filled Denver's heart, gripping it like an iron talon.

Nearly sobbing, Denver gave it up. The horse was nowhere to be found. His only chance was to somehow get the gold back into camp without Sculls knowing it. With that desperate thought burning his mind, Denver rushed back across the rocks, the brush tearing at his flesh.

Gone!

The gold was gone. But it couldn't be gone! Denver threw back his head, wanting to laugh, to cry, to shout profane curses, yet he was frozen to silence.

Again he searched the brush. It had been there. Right there! Dawn flushed the skies a pale rose hue. It took him but a moment to decide.

It was run or die. Denver ran.

* * *

The sunlight in his eyes roused Sculls from his deep sleep. Sitting slowly, he rubbed at his eyes, his tongue filling his mouth with a stale, swollen bitterness. It was thirst, he realized, and he reached for the canteen, cursing as he found it empty. Angrily, he hurled it away.

"Sam!" he shouted.

Sculls drew on his boots and stamped into them. "Denver!" he called again, cupping his hands around his mouth. Thomas was lying near the mesquite tree, dead eyes open to Sculls.

Suddenly it hit him and Sculls wheeled around, his eyes sparking with anger. *No!* His suspicions were confirmed immediately. Denver was gone . . . the gold was gone.

In a rage, Sculls tramped around the campground, screaming curses against Denver, his soul and his lineage.

Pistol in hand, he followed the drag marks in the soft sand, but he lost them among the sumac and manzanita. Beginning again, Sculls swept through the area, his lips frothing slightly as he worked, muttering all the time. Denver had the gold—but how far did the fool think he could run, dragging that weight, before Sculls caught up?

What had made Sam Denver take leave of his senses?

Sculls pulled up short suddenly, groaning mentally as he saw it. The clear, recent hoofprint of a horse in a small clearing. Then another.

Sculls was no tracker and he could not tell that this horse carried no gold and no rider. He only knew that Denver had dragged that trunk up to where a horse was waiting . . . and was now long gone.

Sculls plunged into the deep brush, the rising sun in his eyes, sweat raining into them. The brush tugged at his clothing as he tried to crest the knoll, attempting to cut off the route Denver would be traveling.

Once the man was out of that brush, with a horse . . .

Sculls ran on, breath torturing his lungs by the exertion. His lame knee was shot through with pain. The sun grew hotter, the brush thicker. Deer flies bit furiously at his flesh and the rocks underfoot tore at his boots.

He crested the knoll, searching the empty land, catching no sight of Denver which puzzled him. Panting, the gun in his hand heavy as an anvil, the sun like a branding iron on his back, Sculls tripped down the slope, leaping back as he startled a rattlesnake.

Soon the path became easier, the brush thinning as he worked toward the flats. And there—just in front of his eyes—were the tracks of a horse. Sculls smirked scornfully and increased his pace, jogging down the slope, his heart pumping vigorously, legs wobbly.

Then he heard the nickering of a nearby horse and the hammer of his Colt went back as Sculls began stalking.

He crept across the red dusty earth, moving

152

toward a pile of nopal-studded boulders where the horse had whinnied. The pistol was reassuring in his hand, the sun deadly hot.

The horse, a tall gray, stood there cropping grass. Its head lifted at Sculls' approach.

"Howdy, Sculls," a voice from above him said mildly.

Sculls' head swiveled slowly upward, toward the rocks. The dead man was there, rifle across his knees. A tall, sandy-haired man with blue-gray eyes and a deadly set to his mouth.

Sixteen

Sculls stood petrified, staring into the unblinking sun at Crutcher who perched above him on the rocks like some demonic bird of prey.

"You didn't kill me," Crutcher said, as if to convince Sculls that he was no specter.

"It was you!" Sculls said, his eyes lighting weirdly. "You took the horses, not no damned Indians."

"That's right."

"What'd you do then—feed one to Denver as bait? Take it back when he went after the gold?"

"I did." Crutcher's hat was tipped back slightly, and damned if he wasn't smiling! But Sculls didn't care for that smile a bit.

"You can ride back with me," Crutcher offered, "and let them hang you. Or," he shrugged, "you can take it here. Personally, I'd like to see them hang you . . ." his voice grew ugly, "once for every good man you murdered."

Sculls' face was set, scowling darkly. He had his pistol in his hand still and he measured the man above him. Crutcher had his rifle across his knees as he sat there, and it would only take a squeeze of the tall man's trigger finger—if it were accurate.

"Of course," Crutcher taunted him, "if you take it here, you've always got a chance. A chance for all of it. You've got no chance against a rope."

"That's about the same way I've got it figured," Sculls agreed. Still his brain was working feverishly. If he could step quickly to Crutcher's left, bringing his pistol up at the same time . . .

His thoughts became frantic action and Sculls made his move. He took a rapid, downward step to his left, going to a knee as he brought his Colt up. *Damn the man—he was still smiling!*

Sculls' thought focused on one single point, the man's heart. He had one aim—to erase that damned smile from Crutcher's lips.

Yet it was all wrong and he knew it. The sun was hot in his eyes, the smell of gunsmoke drifted into his nostrils. The horse shied away, kicking angry heels up.

And Crutcher was smiling.

"The hell with that . . ." Sculls muttered, but the gun was missing from his hand. His knee wobbled and his eyes opened suddenly wide.

155

That was blood on his shirt front, a torrent of hot blood! He tried to get to his feet, but his leg wouldn't support him.

At once he felt the shock tear through his body, and—belatedly—heard the roar of the shot Crutcher had fired. Time became frozen, then speeded up incredibly, the world spinning, filled with dust and blood . . . and the pain!

He was on both knees now and, clutching his chest, he looked up at Crutcher. The smile was gone—replaced by a tight bitterness.

"You weren't worth much, Sculls," Crutcher said.

Sculls nodded, gripped his chest still more tightly, and pitched forward, dead.

Conejo wasn't much of a town, but it had the railroad now, and it had civic pride. The town fathers had shut down the only saloon in town, and the men were forced to do their drinking in the back of the general store. Conejo had closed the saloon, gotten rid of the riff-raff and undesirable women, the gambling tables, and as a result they had few visitors. It was an occasion when a stranger rode into Conejo these days and the townfolk stood on the boardwalks of the dusty little street watching the tall man in buckskins lead his string of horses down toward the depot office.

Crutcher swung down from the back of the gray and hefted the heavy box from the buckskin's back, marching into the Southern

156

Pacific office, trunk on his shoulder.

"Who's in charge here?" Crutcher demanded of the little man out front.

"I am!"

Crutcher turned to see a big man with a walrus mustache, a cigar poked into his beefy face. He nodded and dropped the trunk to the floor where it shook the floorboards.

The big man's eyebrows lifted as he poked his thumbs into his vest pockets. The clerk stood, ashen, to one side.

"Name's Crutcher," he told the Southern Pacific men.

Then he pulled his pistol from his holster. The big man, bemused, stood his ground, but the little one ducked behind the counter. Crutcher put the muzzle of the Colt on the strongbox lock and pulled the trigger, blowing the hasp away.

Crutcher holstered his gun and crouched, flipping the strongbox lid open. The gold, in neat sacks, sat there.

Crutcher glanced up at the big man whose eyes were open some now.

"This is the gold Thumb took from the train on its way to Fort Bowie. Think you can take better care of it this time?"

The big man, who had run some rough trails in his life, merely nodded.

"Good." Crutcher dipped into one of the sacks and took out two double eagles which he pocketed. "I need a few things. This is an advance on the reward," he explained. "I want a receipt for this, and I'll want to add a note to Colonel Hodgett."

"All right," the big man said, "if you'll step back here. Higgins!" he called to the little man, "get us some security, and get Mister Crutcher a drink of water."

Higgins nodded and scampered away while the big man scratched out the papers. He glanced up at Crutcher, still chomping on the cold cigar.

"What's your first name, Mister Crutcher?"

"It's been a long time since anybody asked me that," Crutcher answered. "Give me a piece of paper—I'll write it down."

The railroad man read what Crutcher wrote, shook his head and commented, "No wonder you keep it quiet." He folded up the receipt which Crutcher glanced at and tucked away.

"I guess that's about all."

"Where are you going now, Mister Crutcher?" the big man asked as they walked into the outer room where Higgins stood, glass of water in his hand, two shotgun-armed men with him.

"Reckon I'll go get Thumb now," Crutcher said, drinking the water down in three swallows. "Obliged." He handed the glass back to Higgins and was gone.

"What did he say . . . *Thumb?*" Higgins laughed. "He must have been kidding."

"I don't think so. I don't think that man was kidding a bit." The big man shook his head and walked back to his office, lighting the cigar.

What Crutcher had told them was not exactly true. It was not Thumb he was after, but the boy. He still could not find any malice in his heart toward Thumb.

Thumb had killed and had had his own people killed. He was a great warrior whose time had passed by. The times had shifted like the sand beneath his feet, and Thumb and his kind were doomed. Doomed from the moment the horse and gun found their way to this vast, sprawling land.

Crutcher had no sympathy for Thumb, however; he had sorrow for those who would come after and never know the old ways as Thumb had.

He and Thumb were no different, really. After all—whose world had not changed and changed rapidly with the telegraph, the railroads, the self-contained cartridge, the westward spread of the whites? Men who had formerly been inclined to backstep at the sight of their own shadows were now proudly riding the western lands.

It all changes—Crutcher's world, Thumb's world.

Perhaps only the desert is unchanging, mocking man, feared by him, fragile yet awesome in its grandeur, overcoming all incursions in time. Perhaps that was why Crutcher loved it, why he belonged there.

He had his pack horse, the buckskin, loaded with ammunition, water, canned goods and flour as he rode from Conejo. Back to the wide desert. Where the fox ran.

Seventeen

Rebecca tapped at the door, but there was no response. Tray in hand, walking with measured steps, she entered the room and went to the man who sat at the window in the high-backed chair.

"I've brought you something to eat," Rebecca said, but Frank Aston did not answer. She placed the tray on a side table while he sat, unmoving, silent.

The colonel was still in his study when she returned.

"How is he?" the old man asked without looking up from his desk.

"The same." Rebecca circled the room nervously, straightening and arranging objects, until finally she stopped before her father, hands planted on his desk. The colonel's eyes flickered to those of his daughter and with a weary shake of his head, Hodgett placed his pen

161

down and stood, coming around the desk to hold Rebecca a moment.

"It's this business with Crutcher," Rebecca said, stepping back, dabbing at her eye. "And, of course, his arm."

"You're right," Hodgett said. The old warrior picked up the letter on his desk and placed it down again. "I thought after he saw Crutcher's note . . . but nothing changed. He's nursing that hatred still, nurturing it to full growth."

Crutcher's note had arrived with the gold. Simply, the scout had said. "Am after Thumb. Keep Rebecca's hopes up."

"He returned the gold," Rebecca said, "yet even that meant nothing to Frank . . ."

"Why should it?" Aston asked from the doorway. He stood there, head slightly tilted, sleeve pinned up. "It's a trick. Crutcher is clever. Most cunning. He realized, of course, that after I returned and told the truth, he would become a hunted man."

"But he . . ." Rebecca interrupted, but Aston held up a hand.

"Now he will return and claim his reward, expecting that his act has bought him clemency. We must not believe him, Colonel!"

"I fail to see . . ." Hodgett began, but his junior officer cut him short.

"Crutcher simply reasoned that half a loaf is better than none, sir. Now, exonerated, he expects to collect his tithe."

"But he says he's gone looking for Richard," Rebecca argued.

162

"He says," Aston scoffed. "I know that man— he tried to kill me. He's probably laughing at us now, sharing Thumb's hospitality."

Hodgett felt strained, suddenly old. Rebecca was pale. She wanted so to believe that Crutcher was still looking, that somehow a lone man had a chance against the Apache. The colonel wanted to believe it as well. He wished also to believe that he had not been so far wrong in his estimate of Crutcher. Yet he could not wholly convince himself. After all, Frank Aston had been there. Had seen his men butchered, had barely escaped himself.

Rebecca swept her fingertips across her eyes in a gesture of uneasiness. She kept going from day to day in the hope, the fervent wish, that somehow Crutcher could find Richard—that somehow he was well. It had been months . . . years, it seemed, since she had pet his angel hair, kissed his ruddy cheeks . . . and now a known butcher had him.

And Aston was convinced that the man in whom she had placed all of her hopes was no better than the butcher.

At that moment, "the butcher" was riding south by west under clouding skies. Crutcher shifted in his saddle from time to time, yet there was no one behind him as there was nothing, no one before him. Just the two horses plodding across an empty salt playa sea toward the rising mesas and foothills to the west.

There was a spire of crumbled red stone

which he used for his landmark off to the south, and as near as Crutcher could figure, that was the Mexican border.

A lone prospector said he had seen Thumb two days earlier.

"I spent the day deep in my mine shaft," the grizzled desert veteran had told him, "and I had the muzzle of that Spencer .56 aimed up that shaft. They came snooping—but maybe they knew there was nothing down there. Or maybe they knew that I *was*. Anyway, they pulled out, taking my mule—for chow, I expect."

The prospector had shown Crutcher the direction Thumb had taken, and it puzzled Crutcher. He was riding at an angle that would take him back to Mexico where the army was out in force, looking for the Chiricahua renegade.

The nights were bitter cold on the flat desert, the days cooler as winter encircled the basin. The morning after meeting the prospector, the pack horse went lame from a barrel cactus and Crutcher had to turn the buckskin loose. Probably it would return to the mine site.

He had been ten days on the trail, and the tinned goods—a delicacy—were growing slim. He needed food, but shooting was out of the question, snaring too slow.

He made do.

Near a dry lake one windy day, when the sand peppered his face like buckshot and clogged his ears and nostrils, Crutcher found a treasure trove. A series of small mounds in the dry pond caught Crutcher's eye and he smiled, knowing that he had his supper that night—desert toads which had burrowed into the sand, waiting the next rain. No Apache ever turned up his nose at such a feast, nor did Crutcher. He dug the hibernating toads up until he had a bucketful and dined fully that cold evening.

The wind whipped into a fury near midnight, the sand splashing across the dark sky. Crutcher sat holding the reins to the gray, back to the wind, kerchief tight over his nose and mouth, eyes tightly shut.

Day came brilliantly, red-lighting the sands. Yet Thumb's tracks had been erased certainly. The wind had covered any trail as nothing else can.

But men travel in one pattern on the desert—from water to water. Crutcher saddled up and began the slow westward trek. There was water in only one place that he knew of in that dismal area, and he hoped that Thumb knew no other.

High on that bulking mesa, called Mesa Lobo, there were hanging gardens produced by constant seeps. A pencil-thin waterfall plunged through the heights past deep green, tangled vines. Monkey flowers flourished along the cliff, and columbine on the ledges.

It was a place to hide, to rest—unless others knew of it. And, Crutcher was reminded, where water is found on the desert, men tend to remember and transmit the information to others.

It was evening of the following day when he

saw them. Crimson-tinted clouds rose high above the mesa in the coolness of evening. The last golden rays of day pierced the clouds. Deep shadows creased the flats.

There were a hundred of them at least. Cavalry of the Mexican Army. It took only a moment for Crutcher to realize with a shudder that, first of all, they were now into Mexico; and secondly, they had a very good idea where Thumb was now. Whether through chance or cunning, they were right on the Chiricahua's heels.

Crutcher slid back to his horse, leading it silently away up the rocky wash, the shadow of the mesa across them.

Now he was in a fix. He could probably circle the Mexican camp without being seen and warn Thumb that they were waiting. Yet Thumb would undoubtedly welcome a chance to kill Crutcher—especially now when he believed that Crutcher had led an army ambush against him in the Abajos.

It was coming dark, a star poking through here and there, the wind picking up for its dusk flurry. Crutcher picked his way across the broken ground, finally pausing on a crest for a breather. The horse blew and shuffled its feet.

"Well?" Crutcher asked the gray which pricked its ears curiously. "What the hell should we do now?"

There was only one answer, of course. Go for Thumb's camp. He still had the boy and the boy must not be caught in a running battle.

He thought for a while of the boy—Richard—knowing how frightened he was. A train wreck, spirited away by a bunch of painted Apaches, hearing no word he understood, dragged from place to place—sometimes through guns.

Crutcher had circled to the western flank of the mesa. There was no visible way up for a horse, so he looped the pony's reins to a scraggly stand of sumac and slung his rifle on his back.

The climb was dangerous in the darkness and, more than once, Crutcher missed a step and tumbled perilously down. His hands were raw, bleeding, his legs knotted when he finally rolled up onto the caprock of the mesa.

It was still. The chill sky was blanketed with stars.

Moving through the hush of night, crouched low to stay beneath the brush, Crutcher worked across the mesa, toward the canyon springs. He saw no fire and had expected to see none.

There might be a guard out, but Crutcher even doubted that. How many braves did Thumb have left? Six, eight? A ragged, weary tribe fighting its way across the bloody desert.

Thumb was even more dangerous now and Crutcher knew it. A man who might live to fight another day may run. One pinned in a corner will die fighting rather than lie down and take it.

Thumb was cornered.

Crutcher slid and scooted down the canyon where the air was considerably cooler, due in

167

part to the water which gurgled merrily through the night. The sound of the moving water covered Crutcher's movement as well and he was grateful for that.

Suddenly he drew up, his leg lifted for another step. There they were—at the base of the first waterfall, rolled up asleep but for one man. Crutcher edged forward, having no plan but desperation.

He pondered it a moment, then told himself: "I'm damn sure not going to try sneaking up on them in the darkness."

Having decided that, he tipped his hat back slightly and walked down the long slope as dawning colored the high mesa, whistling as he approached the Chiricahua camp.

Instantly the blankets were emptied and the braves scattered into the brush along the creek. Crutcher, still whistling, strode into the clearing and squatted by the dead campfire, sampling the roast javelina.

A brave crept toward him, sleep-reddened eyes on Crutcher.

"Needs salt," Crutcher burped. "Howdy, One Tree," he said to the brave.

One Tree did not answer, but stood trembling with an undefined fury. Crutcher stood erect, finishing the last of the roast boar. By now three other men had come out of the shadows of the deep brush. Weary men they were, two with obvious and serious wounds.

"Got any water to wash that down with, One

Tree?" Crutcher asked.

"Crutcher," One Tree said finally. His voice was taut, face set, but Crutcher could not tell if it was astonishment, anger or hatred which colored One Tree's single word.

The other man came forward finally, slipping from the shadows like a muscular, wounded big cat. Thumb, eyes expressing nothing, holding a rifle in his hands, moved to Crutcher and without a word, slapped the butt of his Winchester across Crutcher's jaw, clubbing him to the ground.

"I have seen no man," Thumb said in his native tongue, "who would travel so far, work so diligently to be killed. My brother, Crutcher defies sanity. He has a will toward death."

Crutcher was on his knees, an ugly gash along his cheek. He stood on rubbery legs and Thumb clubbed him down again, driving the muzzle of his rifle against Crutcher's windpipe, then slamming the butt of his gun against his shoulder just beside the neck.

"Stay down. Stay down and die."

"Maybe I'll die, Thumb. But you know me well enough to know I won't stay down."

Crutcher rose again, battered and bleeding, and this time Thumb let him take his feet. The thick-chested Indian stood near Crutcher, his eyes hard, teeth grinding.

"Why do you come? You know you must die."

"I figured." Crutcher tried to grin, but the

169

pain broke it off. His yellow hair hung across his eyes. "I came for two reasons. First—the boy."

"I have no boy," Thumb said, exasperated.

"Hell—tell that to a city man. I saw his tracks, Thumb. You've got him all right, and you'll give him to me."

"No! You have no claim on *this* boy!"

"I have his mother's claim."

"Did you bring more soldiers with you, Crutcher?" Thumb demanded, his chest rising and falling. The brilliant coming sun glossed his hard muscles.

"I didn't bring 'em, but they're here, Thumb. If you gave it a moment's thought, you know I didn't bring men before. They weren't soldiers— just men who wanted gold."

"There are soldiers?" One Tree asked, his face painted with disconsolate pain.

"Mexican army—I'd say a hundred men. I'm not sure they know you're up here. But if they've got one man who knows there's water here . . . they'll damn sure find you, Thumb. And you'll damn sure die."

"No! We will not die. I will not allow it. The people must survive—my people." Thumb's words were harsh, but his mouth was weighted down with tragedy . . . he knew the situation he was in.

"That why you took the boy, Thumb—to make sure *you* survive? To make sure you have a son to carry on?"

"I could have no son of my own," Thumb

said, his eyes dead on Crutcher's.

"I know . . . I saw Yolanda, Thumb."

"Yolanda! How is she, Crutcher? How did it go for her?"

"Her people scorned her. She was an outcast. She became . . . unrespected."

"I am sorry for that. I would have married her if she had born a child."

"That's it, Thumb—can't you see it?" Crutcher demanded, stepping even closer to Thumb until their faces were within a breath of each other. "You do everything that way: you wanted Daniel and so you forced Morning Rain and me to stay. You wanted a wife and you stole Yolanda, carried her off and ruined her life. You wanted a son—and so you kidnapped a frightened young boy.

"You'll ruin that boy's mother's life. She's a fine woman, Thumb. And you'll ruin the boy's life—he'll be killed accidentally, or crippled . . . body or mind.

"Damn it!" Crutcher shouted. "You've always taken whatever you wanted and hated whoever stood in your way. But you can't stalk a wife as you can a deer, Thumb. You can't take a boy as you'd slip a wolf pup from its den. And the truth is—you can't fight against the tide of change. Everything is slipping away, Thumb, only you're dragging an innocent boy with you."

"You are through?"

Crutcher looked at Thumb. The man's face had regained its stoic strength. Nothing

171

Crutcher had said had made an impression.

"Through? Yeah—I reckon. You hate me, Thumb. You want to kill me. But if you ponder it, you'll realize I don't hate you and I never done a thing to you. I just done what I thought was best for my family—and if a man can die for that, well, you best do it."

"Hard man, Crutcher. No one said that you were not a tough man . . . they never said that." Thumb shook his head.

Crutcher stood, blood still leaking from his jaw. Abruptly Thumb spun around, walking away toward his horses, One Tree and the rest of his warriors, leaving Crutcher alone in the grassy clearing.

After a minute, he heard the horses moving through the brush and then there was nothing. Crutcher sagged to a seat on the rocks and took a deep breath, fingering his slashed cheek.

He could not say what caused him to look up, but look up he did and he was there. Standing on a rock, dressed in buckskin, rigid in childish attention, eyes wide.

"Richard!" Crutcher leaped to his feet and the boy flinched.

The kid's flaxen hair was tied back with a scarf, his mouth petrified into a straight, childish frown. He didn't move as Crutcher walked to him, placing a hand on the boy's shoulder.

From above a horse nickered and Crutcher lifted his head to see Thumb sitting his horse on an outcropping beyond the falls. Crutcher lifted a hand in salute, but Thumb did not respond. He simply turned his horse and vanished once again.

"Damn, boy! Your momma is going to be a joyous woman."

But the kid stood there like a statue and when Crutcher's hand fell off his shoulder, he turned and bolted into the brush.

Crutcher had to drag the kid, kicking and scratching, from a tangle of brambles and for a time after that, he kept a grip on him.

"Sit down here," Crutcher panted, sitting Richard on a rock. "Now, you don't know me, boy, and I suppose I'm a fearsome ugly-looking man with this blood on me. But I'm here to take you to your momma—you understand?"

Richard simply stared at Crutcher, his small mouth twisted into a challenge.

"I know you're only six years old, son. And it's been . . . Lord, ten months, ain't it, since you seen your mother? But I'm takin' you home now. And you've nothing to fear."

The boy never said a word. He simply stared at Crutcher, blue eyes hard as flint. Terror does horrible things to a mind . . . and to a child's mind . . .

"Come on," Crutcher said gently. He picked the boy up in both arms and, cradling him, walked down the long canyon, the boy's unflinching eyes on him.

They came upon the soldiers half a mile on.

rode silently past, dust thick in the dry air. Then, hurriedly, he turned and walked down-slope with Richard, circling back to where his gray was tied.

Sitting the boy in front of him, Crutcher rode swiftly eastward, putting a good mile between himself and the mesa. They had slowed to ford a dry creekbed when he heard it—the distant pop-pop of gunfire. Many guns fired many times.

His head swiveled automatically back toward the mesa, but there was nothing to be seen, nothing to be done.

"Giddup," he urged the gray and they rode on more slowly after that, the boy utterly silent, absolutely rigid.

At the hour before sundown, they camped along a dry wash where some scattered willow brush grew and the trunk of a large, dead cottonwood bridged the wash.

"It ain't much," Crutcher said over his pot of stew, "but it's warm and filling." The boy did not respond. He stood, arms folded, watching Crutcher. "I guess your mother'll have some dandy cooking for you . . . maybe a chocolate cake."

The boy turned his back and Crutcher tasted his stew, then put it aside, watching the boy as sunset flooded the desert. Standing like that in his buckskins, the boy looked remarkably like another six-year-old Crutcher had known. He longed to take the slender shoulders of Richard and hug the boy tightly. Yet the kid was a tangle of emotions—fear, hatred, anger, frustration,

176

worried silly. He's due a whuppin' you wouldn't believe."

The commandant smiled amiably, yet his eyes were not convinced. "I have children of my own," the Mexican said in sympathy. "Yet—my children have never run so far away from home."

"He's a little rapscallion," Crutcher replied with gravity. "It ain't the first time he's done this. He dresses up like an Indian and off he goes, playin' at it. He's good enough with snares and such for his age—he always finds plenty to eat . . . but, darnit, boy, you can't keep this up! Your ma's fit to be tied."

"You saw no real Indians?" the officer asked.

"No real Indians. You can't mean there's wild Indians in these parts?"

"Yes, *señor*. The worst of the lot—Thumb. We were riding to the falls to see if perhaps he had camped there."

"Thumb, you say? That beats all."

"Then you saw no Indians, *señor*. You are certain?"

"Mister, if I'd run into Thumb up there, do you think I'd be standing here talking to you—with my hair still planted and all?"

"No," the commandant laughed. "Yet, I would advise you to take your son and leave this area. Also," he confided, "I would plead for some leniency for the boy. After all," the commandant shrugged, turning his bay's head, "we were young also, no?"

Crutcher stood aside as the stream of cavalry

175

Eighteen

Crutcher hesitated only momentarily, then he painted a smile on his face and walked downhill, carrying Richard. The Mexican soldiers sat their horses in straight ranks. Their officer, a heavy man with dark eyebrows and a massive mustache, approached Crutcher, his handsome bay side-stepping.

"Buenos Dias, señor."

"Howdy," Crutcher nodded. The officer frowned, looking up the mesa slope and then back at Crutcher.

"You were up to the waterfalls?" the Mexican asked.

"Sure was."

"And this . . . he is your boy?"

"He is. Little rascal ran away from home—I got a dirt farm up in the Abajos. His ma's wound up tightly in a knot he could not untie for himself. Nor, to his frustration, could Crutcher.

So small a boy, so large a confusion. He hadn't spoken a word yet, nor looked upon anything with a softened glance.

Maybe out of self-protection, he had become Thumb's son in so short a time. Dreading what might happen if Thumb grew angry, the boy had pushed all of his memories aside and obeyed Thumb's will. Crutcher could not know if any of that was so, was reasonable. He only knew that a small heart, bound up in iron strap, lay within that slender boy.

"Richard." Crutcher called the boy, but he would not turn back.

"Richard." He spoke again, but his voice was different, squeaky, teasing. "Richard."

Tentatively the boy turned his head and then his eyes opened wide. Crutcher sat there before him, yet with Crutcher was an old and trusted friend. Richard started to step forward, but halted, heart pounding.

"You're a naughty boy," Crutcher said, holding that goggle-eyed, grinning puppet up behind his hand. Crutcher wriggled a finger and the puppet waved a reproaching hand at Richard.

"You didn't come back for me, Richard. That was very naughty."

The boy's lip began to tremble and his little wooden face collapsed suddenly into grief, hot tears streaming down his cheeks. He started toward Crutcher hesitantly and Crutcher was to him in a moment, holding him tightly, gently giving the puppet to Richard who turned it over, touching it to his face. The sun was gone now, only a last purple light in the skies.

Crutcher stood there a long moment, rocking the boy, speaking softly to him as the boy trembled with sobbing, until a quiet darkness filled the desert. When Crutcher rolled up to sleep, the boy crawled in with him under the blanket, and Crutcher smoothed back the kid's flaxen hair, holding him as Richard fell off to a quiet sleep, clutching the puppet.

Crutcher watched the far stars and pondered upon it, a slow warmth filling his own stony heart. "It's a wonder," he told himself, "purely a wonder."

Crutcher was up in the cold light of dawn, boiling his coffee. Sleepy-eyed, dazed, Richard crawled out of the blanket and automatically sat beside Crutcher on the fallen cottonwood.

"Coffee ain't much good for kids," Crutcher said, "but I guessed you might like a cup this morning."

Richard nodded and as Crutcher handed him the cup, he managed a "Thanks."

"We'll start riding early. It'll be three days to the nearest town, Conejo."

"All right." Richard sipped at the coffee and glanced with surprise at the cup.

"Ain't much good, I reckon. Sorry I don't carry sugar."

"It's warming," the boy said.

Crutcher saddled the gray and tied down his roll. Then he hefted Richard onto the saddle and slid up behind him.

"You handy with horses?" Crutcher asked.

"Some," the boy answered.

"Want to try this one?" Crutcher handed Richard the reins. "I've got to know this gray pretty good. Now he likes to have his head . . . don't care for a tight rein, but if you give him his head too much he wanders and fights the bit. You got to take him with a sure, but soft hand. Think you can do it?"

"I'll try, sir."

"Good." Crutcher kneed the gray and it moved briskly forward. Crutcher watched the boy, intent on the reins, trying to handle them as Crutcher had instructed him and it warmed his heart to see the childish concentration.

"You've got him figured fine," Crutcher complimented him, patting his shoulder.

"Ain't much to it," Richard said proudly.

"Once you get to know the animal. But they're all different, Richard, like folks. Some'll take to a soft hand, others need to be prodded some. I guess most folks are like this gray— they'll take the easiest road until they're reminded that they're straying."

There was water running off the Abajos into Finger Creek and they nooned on the creek, in the shade of a tall sycamore.

"You know," Crutcher said around a mouthful of bread, "I'll bet you a dollar to a donut there's trout in this creek."

179

"Right now?" Richard asked, animated with enthusiasm. He was on his knees beside Crutcher who was propped up on one elbow, munching the sourdough.

"Yep, right now."

"I'd like to fish 'em . . . but we don't have the goods," Richard said dejectedly.

"Oh, we got the goods," Crutcher said, and the boy's face brightened.

"Think we got the time, Mister Crutcher?" he asked excitedly.

"Ain't much point in hurrying now, is there? Let's give it a try. Cut us some willow rods. I got twine and I reckon this sourdough might appeal to 'em."

"But hooks . . ."

"Son, I always got a couple. It's as necessary to me as ammunition or water out here. Think I'd find me a bass hole or a nice stream like this and pass it up—not on your life."

They fished in close to the shadow of the sycamore which rustled pleasantly in the breeze and within ten minutes, Crutcher had a pan-sized speckled trout. Not fifteen minutes later, Richard pulled one up and his face was aglow with an excitement worth more than all of that gold men had fought over, struggled for.

They stayed on for lunch, frying up their string. Crutcher siestaed, hat tipped low over his eyes, peeking now and then at Richard who skipped stones across the narrow creek and chased down an elusive bullfrog in the cattails.

Two days following, they hit Conejo, riding

180

double the length of the main street.

"Head him into that livery, Richard," Crutcher said. "I reckon it's time to sell this old gray horse off. We'll take the train to Bowie."

"Sell him!" Richard pulled the horse up suddenly. "But we can't, Crutcher. He brought us this far. Can't we ride to the fort?"

"What is it?" Crutcher asked. "It ain't the horse."

"The train . . ." Richard was petrified. "I . . . can't ride it. The last time I rode a train . . . it was terrible. The crash."

"I know." Crutcher slipped from the saddle and stood, studying the boy seriously. "But you got to try it again. Good things can happen on a train, too. It's the quickest way to get you back to your mother, and the most comfortable."

"We've been having such a good time on the trail," Richard pleaded, eyes wide.

"We have. And we'll do it again—I'll promise you. But you got to face up to fear, Richard. A man just has to." Crutcher was serious as he spoke. "If you give in to fear once, you'll give in twice. I don't mean a man shouldn't be scared. Simply that you've got to fight it. If you don't, you'll spend life fighting against yourself."

From across town, the whistle of the locomotive blew shrilly and Richard glanced that way, then looked square at Crutcher.

"I reckon you're right," he said.

They sold the gray for ten dollars, and with that money plus what gold he had left, Crutcher

181

got Richard a reluctant haircut and dressed him in a townboy's suit which the kid regarded with disgust. There was change left for a lunch of steak, apple pie and milk . . . and two first-class tickets to Fort Bowie.

Nineteen

It was a gray, early morning when the hissing, puffing locomotive towed the short string of cars into the Bowie Station. There was no one on the platform but a sleepy-eyed teamster awaiting a load of freight when Crutcher stepped off, Richard beside him.

Hot steam rolled across the platform momentarily, and then the locomotive was shut down. It would be a four-hour layover for the railroad crew.

"You're home," Crutcher said. And if Richard, eyes wide, could hardly believe it, neither could Crutch.

Smoke rose from Bowie and from Cheer, beside it. From upstreet a dog barked and the smells of breakfast drifted through the lazy morning. As they walked out onto Front Street, a hay wagon clattered past and three red-eyed cowhands, sitting their ponies casually, drifted eastward.

"It's big, noisy," Richard said, holding Crutcher's hand.

"Not like out on the desert," Crutcher agreed. He thought of the clean, empty spaces. The burning heat of the days, the bitter cold of the nights. The flights of doves winging across sundown skies . . . a bottle crashed against the floor inside Arizona Sam's saloon.

"Come on," Crutcher said. "Let's get you home."

Richard stood there a moment, however, his hat straight on his freshly barbered head.

"Will it be home now, Crutcher?"

After the desert, would it be? Crutcher smiled and patted the kid's shoulder.

"It'll be home—your mother's there."

Richard nodded and walked forward, Crutcher's hand still resting on his shoulder. Now they could see the walls of the fort ahead of them, hear the piercing commands of an early morning drill. They had almost passed the man before Crutcher recognized him.

Ivory Hunter stepped out of the shadows of the blacksmith's shop and called him.

"Crutch."

"Ivory . . . so you healed up!" Crutcher took the old scout's hand fondly. Ivory shook it warmly and nodded at the kid.

"This can't be . . . is it Richard?" Ivory asked.

"It is. And he's a fine young man. Richard, this here's Ivory Hunter—friend of the Indians

184

and of mine."

"Damn, Crutch . . . ! You actually did it." Ivory shook his head in wonder.

"With a little luck." He looked at Ivory, not wanting to ask it, but Ivory Hunter guessed his thoughts.

"Yolanda's in Cheer. Working in the mercantile store. It's with thanks to her that I've recovered so well. She's a fine nurse, Crutch. A fine woman."

"I'll have to drop in some time," Crutch said, his face expressionless. "I'm happy to hear she's doing fine."

"She's tryin' to put her life back together. My guess is she'll make it," Ivory Hunter said.

They were in the shadow of the fort before it seemed to finally hit Richard and his legs trembled as he stopped, holding Crutcher back. There were tears in his eyes.

"You've got to go in with me," the kid begged.

"Sure I will," Crutcher answered.

The gate was open and the sentry merely glanced at the tall man in buckskins and the kid in the new gray suit, yet they had only gotten halfway across the parade ground before the greeting got considerably more spirited.

She was on the porch of the colonel's office, sitting in the morning sun, rocking in her rocking chair when she saw them. Rebecca came to her feet, hands going to her mouth in astonishment. She took a hesitant step forward, then rushed down onto the parade ground and,

185

in a moment, she had Richard enfolded in her arms and they were both crying, murmuring soft reassurances.

Crutcher stood aside, hat in his hands, as the colonel, hatless, sleeves rolled up, appeared on the porch, led by his sergeant.

"Richard!"

The hatless, silver-haired colonel was to them in six quick strides, hugging them both in his massive arms, eyes filled with tears. Finally, he stood and fixed those eyes on Crutcher.

"Crutcher. Damn, man . . . we never believed . . . never dared believe."

"I can hardly believe it myself, Colonel. It was God's good luck brought us through."

"I'm sure," Hodgett said. "But I'm as sure that you had something to do with it yourself. Come inside, I want to hear about it. What happened to Thumb?"

"I can't say for a fact," Crutcher said as they went into the colonel's office, followed by Richard and Rebecca. "He got into a scuffle with the Mexican army. There were a lot of shots being fired. I think he's probably dead. If not, he's hardly got a force left."

"I'll have some coffee brought up, Crutcher—there's a few details left to consider. If you could stand some coffee."

"I could stand it, sir," Crutcher smiled.

"Good. Come on, Richard," Hodgett said, picking up the boy and placing him on his back. "While we're down there, we'll see if Corky has some of those cookies left."

Crutcher was left standing in the sunlit room with Rebecca, his hat in his hands.

"I still can't believe it," she said. "He looks so fine."

"He's a fine boy, ma'am. If you don't mind, I told him I'd come back and see him some time. Take him fishing."

"You'd be welcome, Mister Crutcher. Most welcome." Without warning she raised on tiptoes and kissed Crutcher on his unshaven cheek. "I can't thank you enough. Come back any time you've a mind to."

She withdrew from him and it was only then that Crutch was the silhouette in the inner doorway. He took a step forward, and Crutcher recognized Aston.

But he was a changed man. His eyes were sunken, his uniform rumpled. There was a big Colt Dragoon pistol in his hand and he lifted it without a word and fired.

Smoke filled the room and Crutcher felt a bullet slam into him. Aston started to lift that hogleg again, but Crutcher stepped to him, slapped him viciously across the mouth and wrenched the pistol from him, hurling it through the window, shattering glass.

Men were rushing toward the room now, Hodgett bursting through the door. Crutcher had a hand to his shoulder. The bullet had dug through it clean, just beneath the collarbone, ruining a perfectly good buckskin shirt and taking a fair-sized chunk of meat in the bargain.

"He's a killer," Aston raved. "A killer. Take

him out men. Execute him."

Hodgett nodded to the troopers and they backed out of the room.

Rebecca slid Crutcher's shirt from his back and he stood there, bare-chested, facing Aston.

"Lieutenant, I don't know what's taken seed in your mind and taken root there . . ." he winced as Rebecca cleaned the wound.

"You have, Crutcher. You. You killed my men. Tried to kill me."

"That's not true."

"He's been saying it since he returned," Hodgett put in. "I guess you'll have to answer this accusation sooner or later, Crutcher. Want to do it now?"

"I do, sir. Aston—you think I wanted to kill you. Now listen to me. When you were shot, you went out cold. When you came to, you were buried under a pile of pine needles, weren't you?"

"Yes, but . . ."

"I know because I dragged you there and piled 'em over you so you couldn't be found. You were on the north side of the camp, down a narrow gulley about fifty feet, with pine needles covering you. Now that's the truth, ain't it?"

Aston had to admit it was.

"All right. Seeing as I wanted to kill you so much, why didn't I? Since I knew right where to find you. No, Lieutenant Aston, it was me put you there for safekeeping under them pine needles."

Crutcher was mad enough to shake, and the

pain was hot in his shoulder. Richard was there, trembling as he held his grandfather's leg.

"I guess . . ." Aston began.

"I'll be leaving," Crutcher said. Maybe Aston would come around to being the man he had once been, maybe not. But just then Crutcher decided he had had enough of the army and all its people for a good long while. He walked stiffly to Richard and solemnly shook his hand.

"You're a good man, Richard. Remember what I told you. One of these fine days, we'll go fishing together and that's a promise."

"I'll summon the camp doctor," Hodgett said, starting toward the door.

"No, sir. That's all right. The bullet passed on through. I need some rest and some nursing, but I think I know where I can find me a good nurse." Crutcher nodded and stepped out into the sunlight, Rebecca and Hodgett watching from the porch as he walked back toward Cheer, holding his shoulder.

"There goes a man," Hodgett said quietly. Then they turned and went in. Richard lingered a moment and then followed.

It was Ivory Hunter who scurried off to get Yolanda and together they helped Crutcher to her room above the mercantile.

She bustled busily about the room, gathering her bandages, basin and scissors. Crutcher smiled through the pain as he sat in the lone chair of the small room.

She looked fine. The puffiness was gone from

her face, the powder paleness of her cheeks restored to a rosy health.

"I worried so for you, Crutcher, when you did not come back." She tenderly removed the rest of his shirt and clucked at the sight of the wound. Ragged, it was, and bloody, but it should leave him with nothing more than an occasional stiffness.

"I was thinking some of you too," Crutcher said.

Yolanda glanced at him and blushed faintly.

"No," she said.

"Sí. You look well," he told her as she tightened the bandage.

"I have been doing well," she agreed, wiping back an errant strand of dark hair. Suddenly she stopped and stared at Crutcher whose eyes were clear, his face tanned and lean.

"And you, Crutcher—you look different as well."

"I feel different." Crutcher stood and slipped into a clean white shirt Yolanda had brought from the mercantile. He walked to the window, standing there only a minute.

"It was the boy," he confided, sitting on the window sill. "After Daniel, I thought I could never again enjoy being around a boy. I thought it would hurt too much. But that Richard, he's a good boy, Yolanda. It almost made me think . . ."

Yolanda turned her back sharply and Crutcher watched her shoulders, the raven hair on the base of her neck. She busily cleaned the basin until Crutcher's hand went to her shoulder. He turned her slowly toward him and there was a tear in her eye.

"After Morning Rain died, I thought I'd never be able to think of another woman . . . now I'm thinking of one, Yolanda."

"But I have . . ." she objected, but he shushed her.

"I'm asking you to marry me, Yolanda."

"But, Crutcher!" She turned down her eyes, but he lifted her chin.

"I mean it. I'll have some money coming now. I've been thinking of settling up in the Abajos, out on that golden desert. It could be fine, Yolanda. Maybe I'll have another son one day," he said softly, and Yolanda threw her arms around his neck, tears trickling down her cheeks as she kissed him. Crutcher winced and gasped, laughing. Yolanda drew back—she had forgotten about his shoulder and had been squeezing him with all her might.

"I don't think love has to hurt *that* bad," Crutcher said, and she laughed again, burying her head against his chest.

"But, Crutcher . . ." she said, stepping back. "I can't marry you." He looked at her curiously, eyebrows knit. "I don't even know your first name," she explained.

"No. I realize that . . ." he stammered and color rose to the tips of his ears. "Come here. Come closer," Crutcher said, and she did. He glanced around the room and then whispered something into her ear.

191

"No!" she laughed, pushing back. Crutcher nodded solemnly.

"I will never tell a soul," she said. "But, Crutcher! *I* must name the children!"